T4-ALI-574

LADY IN HARLEY STREET

It seems the answer to all Dr Celia Derwent's prayers when her new boss Dr Alan Grainger proposes marriage. She desperately wants to convince the courts that she should have custody of her orphaned niece Fiona, and with a husband she will stand a far better chance of persuading them. Alan is devoted to Fiona, but he still seems aloof and strangely wary of Celia. So will this marriage of convenience really solve all her problems?

WITHDRAWN

LARGE PRINT
MAINE STATE LIBRARY
STATION 64
AUGUSTA, ME 04333

LADY IN HARLEY STREET

Anne Vinton

FEB 8 1989

ATLANTIC LARGE PRINT
Chivers Press, Bath, England.
John Curley & Associates Inc.,
South Yarmouth, Mass., USA.

Library of Congress Cataloging in Publication Data

Vinton, Anne.
  Lady in Harley Street / Anne Vinton.
    p.   cm.—(Atlantic large print)
  ISBN 1–55504–720–3 (pbk. : lg. print)
  1. Large type books.   I. Title.
[PR6072.I54L34 1989]
823′.914—dc19

88–21021
CIP

British Library Cataloguing in Publication Data

Vinton, Anne
  Lady in Harley Street.
  I. Title
  823′.914[F]

  ISBN 0–7451–9425–7

This Large Print edition is published by Chivers Press, England, and John Curley & Associates, Inc, U.S.A. 1989

Published by arrangement with Harlequin Enterprises B.V.

U.K. Hardback ISBN 0 7451 9425 7
U.S.A. Softback ISBN 1 55504 720 3

© Anne Vinton 1965
Australian copyright 1983
Philippine copyright 1983

LADY IN HARLEY STREET

All the characters in this book have no existence outside the imagination of the Author, and have no relation whatsoever to anyone bearing the same name or names. They are not even distantly inspired by any individual known or unknown to the Author, and all the incidents are pure invention.

CHAPTER ONE

Celia thought, 'I hate parties. Hate, hate, hate parties, and I wish I was at home.'

The noise was deafening. Not only was there music, to which nobody was paying much regard, but the buzz of conversation, reaching one who was already tired to the point of exhaustion by the day's events, and worried sick into the bargain by private problems, sounded like several thousand bees doing overtime and made one's head ache. It was even worse listening to the laughter. Women's laughter was mostly shrill and inane or throaty, like a gargle.

'I'm not feeling at all generous towards my fellows this evening,' Celia mused. 'The fault lies in me. When one isn't in a party mood one shouldn't come to parties, and I've never felt less like a party in my life.'

Reggie had said, however, as they shared their morning coffee at eleven-thirty, 'I particularly want you to come to the Bennistons' tonight, Celia. They're having a party. There's something I want to get off my chest, and I simply never seem to have a minute with you nowadays.'

Celia had protested, 'Oh, Reggie, I hate that sort of party. Couldn't we manage a lunch one day?'

1

'Sorry, sweet, I'm booked with grateful and glamorous patients every day in the foreseeable future, I'm afraid. It will have to be the Bennistons, if you have any love for me at all.'

This was lightly said and as lightly taken, though Celia knew that Reggie expected her to be at the party without further question. She had no idea what it was he wished to discuss with her. He was a busy and popular specialist, though his speciality took the form of general medicine with a certain emphasis on the activities of the glands, and Celia had been his assistant for the past six months. Though he was her employer, he was the sort of person who preferred to be called 'Reggie' than insist upon the dignity and deference due to one in his position. To many of his women patients he was also 'Reggie.' He was fairly proficient at his job and extremely successful socially. Hostesses adored his rapier-sharp wit and experienced gallantries; he was handsome, mature and a bachelor; all points in his favour. Celia genuinely liked him. He was invariably amusing without ever being unkind and was the same person outside his consulting room as in it.

Celia felt she was lucky to be working for someone like Reggie for such a princely salary. She had enjoyed working in hospital, perhaps more than in exclusive practice, but suddenly had come the need to earn more than the Hospital Board was prepared to pay her; suddenly had come tragedy with the deaths of Les and Belle in their small secondhand car. Les was Celia's younger, only brother and had been married since he was twenty-one. Their child, Fiona, then two and a half years old, had been thrown clear and was miraculously uninjured.

Friends of Celia's had looked after Fiona until the double funeral was over, but temporary arrangements were useless in providing for a growing child. She had to know the security of love before she could realise she was bereft. Automatically she had turned to her aunt, and Celia, battening down the grief of her own loss, determined that Fiona should not be the loser if she had any say in the matter.

Within a month she had her new job with regular hours so that she could see Fiona for an hour each morning before she left for Harley Street, and again at five-thirty each evening, also weekends and Thursday afternoons. She had taken over the lease of her brother's flat in South Kensington and so Fiona returned to her own home with scarcely any comment. Once or twice she asked where her mummy and daddy were, but she was too young to know what death meant and accepted the fact that they had 'gone away' on the assurance that 'Aunty C' was there to stay. Celia employed a young widow with a

3

small child of her own to come in every day and look after Fiona. The two children played together, quarrelled regularly and established a firm, normal friendship. Previously Fiona had been rather a lonely child as there were no other tots in the same house and fraternisation was rarely encouraged in this part of London in any case. Celia felt she now had an ideal arrangement and a ready-made child whom she adored. Her work was for Fiona, which was why she refused to regret the hospital, and her future was also dedicated to her niece. Fiona would eventually board at a good school and be given every encouragement to work to enter one of the professions, if she desired her independence as Celia herself had done.

Perhaps Dr Celia Derwent did not consciously acknowledge that since she had taken over her brother's child something else had ceased to trouble her, as it had always done during her solitary hours and at times in her dreams. Celia was very pretty for such an erudite young woman; her figure was on the small side, but her natural poise made her appear taller than she really was; her hair was the colour of a ripe chestnut and grew like a cap around her elfin face. Her eyes were wide and a clear grey; her lashes surprisingly long and dark. Such as she was she could not have failed to make many a masculine heart beat faster, especially during her years at medical

4

school, but Celia had confined herself to looking back encouragingly at only one of these, Tony Crawley, who was in his fifth and final year when she met him after a rugby match at the beginning of her second.

She had fallen in love with Tony as she had never loved before nor expected to do again. So stormy and emotional had been their brief encounter that it was almost a relief, albeit a painful one, when Tony had qualified and moved on to walk a hospital's wards for the required year before branching out into private practice. Then letters were exchanged, letters so tender and revealing that they were almost better than being together in that one could enjoy the emotion without the distractions of the presence. For six months the affair continued to blaze like a bright, promising flame, and then Tony began to default. At first an expected letter from him didn't materialise and when it did, eventually, it was filled with apologies rather than warmer sentiments. After a month of this uncertainty Tony didn't write for three full weeks at a stretch. Celia wanted to write, asking him in a kind of panic what was happening to all the warmth and security she had felt from their love, but she forbade herself this indulgence and made herself work the harder, so that she came top in an anatomical examination which was held about that time. When Tony eventually did write it

5

was to tell Celia that he had been seeing a lot of a very pretty blonde nurse from the Casualty Department of his hospital and that 'tempus fugited' whether one wished it to or not and had she, also, forgotten him a little?

Celia replied, before she could have time to think, that as they were not engaged she supposed they were both free to see whomsoever they wished and that their careers, she again supposed, were of paramount importance at the moment in any case.

Tony did not write again until a card and a dozen pink roses arrived the day after her birthday in November. His next communication was a Christmas card, and that was the absolute end of the affair. Celia suffered a good deal from it, of course. She lost a lot of her feminine confidence, and when other young men attempted to restore it for her, she was such a passive partner in these essays that they didn't ask her out again, feeling rebuffed by her lack of response and moody mien.

The first fine careless rapture, she was convinced, could never be recaptured. Tony had been her great love and she had lost him. A lesser relationship could not be for her. She would prefer to be a good, unmarried career woman than a wife who was scooping up the crumbs from a banquet upon which others had feasted. Occasionally news came to her of

6

Tony from acquaintances of his she still knew. He hadn't married the blonde nurse. Tony was heard of in Stockport and, later, as the junior of a big 'firm' in Essex. Celia felt that he, too, had found nothing to match that great love of theirs and must occasionally hanker after her. If he did then he would want her back one day and find her waiting. She often thought of the moment of reunion and how it would all be the same and without recriminations.

At times when she faced the truth she told herself that Tony hadn't wanted her, didn't want her and would never want her. What he had wanted was the nearest available pretty girl and she had just happened to be that girl at the time. That she had put her heart into it was her misfortune and not really his fault. Now that she knew how men were she could be much more wary and understanding of their weaknesses.

She grew out of much of her disillusionment and the hurt to her pride as time went on and she in turn qualified and then took her MD degree for good measure. She found she could believe in love again, and even hoped it would happen to her once more. It hadn't done to date, however, and a certain measure of disappointment troubled her solitary moments. Then there had been the tragedy and Fiona was suddenly in her arms, wanting love as Celia was anxious to dispose of it. It began to look like a most amicable arrangement, providing there were no hidden snags to being an unmarried foster-mother. After almost six months it appeared safe to assume that no complications would now arise. The child was healthy, normal, loved her aunt and had forgotten her parents, which could only be a blessing for everybody. Later on Celia intended to tell Fiona all about the young couple who had loved, brought her into the world, and then died together. She had kept photographs for this purpose. She felt this should be done only when there was no danger of troubled emotions being aroused by the knowledge, for often there is a sleeping dog left in the subconscious mind after all the conscious ones have long ceased to bark.

Meanwhile lawyers were still busily settling the estate of the deceased couple, who had not anticipated their early demise and so had made no adequate provision for it. Oddments of cash kept turning up from various sources, even a premium bond, which had belonged to Les, had won a five-hundred-pound prize and the beneficiary had to be Fiona, although the accumulated red tape of transferring the benefit simply couldn't be believed. It took lawyers to unravel all the mysteries of their own maze-like world, and when Celia mentioned legal adoption she was asked to wait until other matters had been successfully concluded before presenting them with yet another.

'But there can be no doubt I'll be able to keep Fiona?'

'I should think there can be little doubt, Dr Derwent. There are so few relations to be considered, and everyone doesn't look on the addition of a child to the household as indulgently as you appear to do. We have been approached by the legal representative of Mr Harold Wicheter. He, I believe, was Mrs Derwent's father?'

'The Wicheters adopted Belle when she was nine. They took her out of an orphanage and she lived with them on their sheep station in New South Wales.'

'They would be fairly wealthy people, then?'

'I should imagine so. Why are they in touch with you?'

'I should imagine maybe they wish to contribute to the child's future. They must be considered interested parties.'

'But they objected to Belle's getting married to an English boy, and refused to come over for the wedding. They weren't even writing to Belle any more, after saying things like she had made her own bed and must lie on it. Belle had intended persuading my brother to visit Australia with her one day, but in the face of these things he took a good job in England and they were very

9

happy,' she concluded rather on a note of defiance.

'I don't doubt it, Dr Derwent,' said the lawyer placatingly. 'When shall I tell Mr Hodson he can call and see the child?'

Celia had felt peculiar and nervous when the stranger had been admitted to the flat and had promptly begun to make friends with Fiona. It was a Saturday morning, so neither Mrs Fern nor Billy was present. It was a wet morning in July; so far it had been a rather miserable summer, and Fiona was a little fretful over having their usual trip to the shops delayed until the afternoon. She refused to play even with her favourite toys and her nose was running. It was obvious that she was in the throes of a summer cold.

'She's rather a pale child, isn't she?' asked Mr Hodson.

'All children aren't rosy apples,' Celia told him. 'In any case, we haven't had a lot of sun this summer.'

The man smiled sympathetically.

'I'm an Australian,' he said unnecessarily, 'and I don't know how you Pommies can live without the sun.'

'We manage,' Celia told him quietly.

Fiona began to wail and resisted when Celia tried to take her up on her lap. She also wet her pants, something she hadn't achieved in the daytime for some months. After dealing with the situation Celia was quite pink from her exertions.

'This must be a strain for you, Dr Derwent,' Hodson proceeded. 'You do work, don't you?'

'Yes. But I have a woman coming in five days a week. It's no strain. I consider looking after my brother's child a privilege.'

'You and this woman you employ,' the lawyer said slyly.

'I spend a lot of time with Fiona,' Celia said rather sharply.

'I'm sure you do.'

'I changed my job to have more time with her. In my present work I have no night calls or emergencies. I am assistant to a specialist and we work only to appointments.'

'Is that the best thing for you, Doctor? Haven't you rather limited your own career for the sake of this child?'

'What are you trying to say, Mr Hodson? What have you come here to try to prove?'

Lawyer-like, the man drew back his legal identity.

'My clients have asked me to assure myself of the child's well-being, Dr Derwent. Naturally they think of her as their kin—'

'But she isn't really, is she? They haven't interested themselves in her up to now.'

'They have always been interested in their adopted daughter's activities. They were angry and hurt when she acted without consulting them while she was visiting here, thanks to their financial backing, but anger can't stifle natural concern and affection. When the child was born they knew. Pride was beginning to crumble and I know they were planning a surprise visit and reconciliation when the tragedy occurred.'

'What a pity Belle died before she knew that!' Celia exclaimed.

'Anyway, I can tell them the child's in good hands,' the man said, rising and looking out of the window at the small area fronting on to the shabby-genteel street. 'Got no garden?' he asked.

'No. But the park is quite near. On fine days Fiona is taken to the park every day.'

'Parks!' Mr Hodson almost snorted, but as he was by now reaching for his hat Celia forgave him.

She felt relieved when he had gone, but the visit, and the reasons behind it, continued to worry her for a week or two and then she decided nothing else was going to come of it. She had mentioned the matter to Reggie, who said, 'They're bound to show some concern, my sweet. They must feel pangs from old conscience, what, that having cast Belle off from the family she died without knowing that she was forgiven, and all that? They'll probably want to help. You must accept, darling.'

Yesterday, however, on September the twenty-eighth to be exact, the blow she had secretly feared had fallen. Her own lawyers had informed her that the Wicheters wanted to adopt Fiona and bring her up as their own child with all the advantages, both physical and material, of their position as successful sheep-farmers in New South Wales. They had investigated all possibilities as to the child's future and had concluded that her place was with them as her mother's had been. They appreciated Dr Derwent stepping into the breach and would be only too happy to relieve her of the responsibility and the extra work an infant created.

'But I don't want to be relieved,' Celia gasped. 'I want Fiona with me.'

'The courts will now have to make the decision, Doctor,' the lawyer's impersonal voice told her. 'These people may have a strong case. We must be prepared for a fight.'

'I won't let them take her. I won't,' Celia said almost to herself.

'If you were married, or even engaged,' the lawyer proceeded, 'our case might be stronger. In placing a young child the courts like a safe, domestic situation with both foster-father and mother and a settled, stable establishment. As a single woman you will always require to be anxious about your own career.'

'At twenty-five I am expected to be dusty from sitting on the shelf?' Celia demanded bitterly.

13

'Dr Derwent, I am putting this business to you as an impartial justice will see it. Once we know the opposition's strength then we can review our own weakness and see what is to be done about it.'

'I'm sorry,' Celia said stiffly. 'You have your job to do. I suppose I'd better come and see you when convenient?'

'I think you are free on Thursday afternoons? I'll expect you at two-thirty and we can have a long, leisurely chat.'

CHAPTER TWO

With this on her mind Celia did not feel she exactly blended with the party atmosphere around her, and to make her feel even more isolated Reggie was late. She knew as the very good-looking man had a word with their hostess and then came in her direction that he had been told to look after her and, quite unreasonably, she bitterly resented the fact.

'I'm waiting for Dr Marquess, thank you,' she said, before the stranger could even speak to her.

He gave a rather mocking bow and reduced his considerable height—he was about six foot three—so that a pair of very dark eyes looked briefly into her own.

'I'm glad to hear it,' he said with a faint

14

smile. 'Reggie is worth any lady's waiting time. May I replenish your glass without appearing pushy?'

'No, thank you.' She was angry with herself for being so ungracious; angry with the stranger for laughing at her and angry with Reggie for leaving her standing about looking vulnerable among people she didn't care to know.

When Reggie did arrive he made extremely slow progress towards her. Every woman in the room was apparently either his patient or his friend of long standing. She heard him scattering 'darlings' and 'sweets' liberally around. The tall, dark stranger and he shot a few words at one another, but they were not, apparently, great friends, as they both moved away quickly in opposite directions.

When, eventually, Reggie Marquess at last reached Celia sitting behind a concealing rubber plant, he looked a little odd, she fancied, almost uncertain of himself, and Reggie was not one to be uncertain of anything, least of all himself. He had the most supreme self-confidence of anybody she knew.

'I thought you were never coming,' she greeted him, 'and I was so bored.'

'Well, thank you, darling. I take that as a backhanded compliment. Now your boredom has dissipated with my arrival. Well done!'

This was the Reggie she knew, and she

15

smiled faintly.

'I don't imagine anyone has ever been bored in your company, Reggie, whatever else they may have been.'

He patted her knee chummily.

'Like penicillin, I am allergic to a few, but I shall hope you and they never meet, my love. What are you drinking?'

'I've only had tomato juice. I hate getting tiddly when I'm not even enjoying myself.'

'I shall get you a large pink gin. I insist.'

She sipped the spirit when he returned, wondering what exactly Reggie wanted to say to her. 'Something off my chest,' had been his words to her that morning. Could it be that he wanted her to leave the practice? Wasn't he as happy with their arrangement as he always appeared to be?

She studied his countenance at intervals, trying to assess his mood. He was about forty, though the silver at his temples made him appear more. He had a neat, clipped moustache and bright blue eyes. They always made her think of the Pied Piper of Hamelin. His lips were soft and well shaped, rather like a woman's, but it was a kind face, rather indulgent and—she had to admit it—weak.

He was glancing at her, too, and then at last he spoke.

'Look here, my sweet . . .'

'What is it, Reggie?' she took him up. 'I think you should tell me what's wrong.'

She had wanted to confide in him about the prospect of a court wrangle over the custody of Fiona, but if he wanted to dismiss her it was obvious that he wouldn't wish to hear about her troubles, especially as he would be adding to them.

'I rather thought you wouldn't think of it as wrong, my dear,' he laughed uneasily. 'The fact is I've been viewing our association in a different light recently, and it's been most upsetting. Most upsetting indeed.' He took an almost offended gulp of whisky. 'It's just too ridiculous for words.'

'I don't seem to get the hang of what you're talking about, Reggie. How can our association be viewed differently? What are you trying to say?'

'Celia, my fair one, my world has suddenly toppled. I think I'm in love with you. You're not to laugh.'

'Laugh?' she looked stunned. 'I—I couldn't laugh at a thing like that. I didn't know, Reggie. I never suspected. You have a queer way of falling in love with somebody.'

'That's because I've been fighting it, my dear little love. Reggie Marquess and connubial bliss don't go together. I've loved 'em lightly, never harmed 'em, and let 'em go. Butterfly amours were my forte. You I just never considered in this respect.' He shook his head rather sadly. 'Then I was seeing only you, dreaming about you,

17

watching and listening for your arrivals and departures with bated breath. It's been absolute hell waiting for it to pass,' he added pathetically, 'and now I know there's going to be nothing for it but to conform and ask you to marry me. I can, of course, provide you with every comfort. I shall try to be a good father to the child. I shall lay my considerable world at your dainty feet, my pet, and in return—' he took her hand and kissed it. His eyes had grown strangely dark and brooding—'you will be a great comfort to me.'

'I'll have to think about it,' she murmured. 'This has been such a surprise, Reggie.'

'Of course. Perhaps you'll join me for luncheon at my club tomorrow, and give me your answer then? Of course, I know I'm much older than you, my dear, but I'm young at heart. The idea doesn't disgust you?'

'No, of course not.' She was shocked, amazed, touched by his reference to Fiona, but by no means horrified. She was just beginning to realise that this could be the answer she was looking for. Marrying Reggie would be her answer to the Wicheters. 'May I go home now?'

'Of course. Have you your car with you?'

'No. I left it at the garage with a flat tyre. I'll get a taxi.'

'Rubbish! One moment.'

Reggie went across the room and spoke to

the tall man she had already met, who was also making his farewells.

'Alan will take you home,' he came back to inform her. 'No trouble,' he told her as she protested, 'he goes your way. Sweet dreams, my love.' He kissed her on the cheek and she collected her coat and ran down the stairs in the wake of Alan, feeling as though she would wake up any moment and find she had been dreaming.

'It appears you're being forced into my company willy-nilly,' the amused voice spoke into her thoughts as a still handsome yet elderly Jaguar drew up at the kerb, and admitted her into its warm interior.

'It's very kind of you,' she said in a preoccupied manner, 'I hope I'm not putting you out.'

'Not at all. I live in Knightsbridge.'

'Oh.' She felt annoyed that she had to give this her attention. 'That means you have to redouble. We reach Knightsbridge first. Please drop me where convenient and I'll get a taxi the rest of the way.'

'Not at all. I was asked to see you home and see you home I shall. Reggie was adamant.'

'You know each other, then?'

'Not really. We're acquainted.'

★   ★   ★

Celia scarcely noticed the Jaguar disappearing down the rather shabby street, after she had alighted, so anxious was she to get inside and review the events of the evening. The baby-sitter, a girl who was studying at the local college and was glad of a few hours' solitude in which to work, for which she was also paid, left to walk back to her lodging in the next street and Celia glanced in on Fiona, who was sleeping soundly, put the percolator on the hotplate in the kitchen and sat down on a high stool to think.

Was Reggie's proposal her answer from a benign providence? It certainly looked like it. He might have been listening when the lawyer said, 'If only you were married, Dr Derwent, or even engaged . . . our case would be much stronger.' How sweet of him, too, to promise to be a good father to Fiona. It was a big thing for a man like Reggie, whose personal freedom had always meant so much to him and his way of life, suddenly to want to take on not only a wife but a youngster as well. He must be very much in love to even consider such a step, for he had made it very obvious that he had tried to overcome his passion before it could be allowed to overcome him.

Celia began to feel very tender towards Reggie, who had paid her this supreme compliment and so given her an unwitting assurance that her guardianship of Fiona would be unimperilled.

She wondered briefly what would happen if she turned down his proposal? Would he want her to leave the practice? It was obvious they could not continue working amicably together if there was embarrassment on the one hand and some resentment on the other. But she was not considering turning Reggie down at the moment when the dawning of affection for him was warm in her bosom.

She went off to bed nursing this affection and trying to imagine what life in Reggie's household would be like. Fun, of course. Reggie and fun were synonymous: she would continue to work with him and they would be able to discuss their awkward and frustrating cases far into the night after they had tucked Fiona up in her cot. Her mind baulked a little at the idea of Reggie in the nursery. His urbane presence did not exactly lend itself to romps on all fours or piggy-backs. She supposed he would learn in time and they might even have children of their own. This again was something it was difficult to imagine, so she put it aside and thought kind and convenient thoughts until she slid into the depths of sleep.

The next morning her fondness for Reggie was the first thing which struck her, and then she felt tremendously grateful to him. It would be a privilege to make him happy for all he was doing for her. In this mood, while

Fiona played with her bricks awaiting the arrival of her playmate, Celia typed a letter to her lawyers saying that Dr Marquess, the Harley Street physician, had asked her to marry him and this would obviously put a different complexion on the question of Fiona's guardianship which she would like him to place on record immediately.

She delivered the letter by hand as soon as she had collected her car from the nearby garage, and then began the frustrating struggle to reach Harley Street by ten a.m. while being forced to go at least twelve miles out of her way owing to one-way streets, roads under repair and other everyday hazards.

This gave her time to think and the warm glow at her heart cooled a little as reason held sway. Was this proposed marriage fated to be made in heaven, exactly? She had thought of herself not at all in regard to becoming Mrs Reggie Marquess, save in the context of being Fiona's guardian. Also, in the possibility of refusal, she had thought of herself as Fiona's guardian temporarily doomed to be out of work. As Celia Derwent, woman of flesh and blood and robust desires, she had thought not at all. What was Reggie like as a lover? Could she stand him in this role, after all those admitted conquests of his, no matter how lightly they had been loved and lost? Did she know anything of Reggie's personality save

22

what she knew in regard to their daily partnership, which had never been anything but purely professional? She had, in fact, occasionally regarded Reggie in an avuncular light; he was a sweet uncle who listened sympathetically to one's troubles and then disarmingly dismissed them as not being troubles at all. Could this man rise to the heights of ecstasy she had always told herself were the province of people who were not only in love but communicated their love and made a holy sacrament out of it? If every man was by nature the flint, then she was not the tinder for Reggie, and never could be in a hundred years.

'Stop being so negative,' she chided herself. 'Think what you are and can be to Reggie. You are no longer an eighteen-year-old girl with stars in your eyes.'

But the stars are still in some people's eyes when they are eighty, an inner voice persisted. Think of some of those old ladies on the geriatric ward at St Nick's when their ancient husbands came creaking down the ward to see them at visiting time: one could imagine every one of those bent and wizened old men was Sir Lancelot mounted on a white horse, to judge from the faded, bright eyes of the patients watching their progress.

'I couldn't be satisfied with less than the best,' Celia almost howled, 'so why am I kidding myself? I hate the idea of being an

23

old maid, but at least I'll be an old maid who respects herself. I'll fight for Fiona off my own bat, and if I lose her—well, I suppose I'll get over it, and she'll still have a good life ahead of her. I must tell Reggie it's no, and there it is.'

But Reggie was proving elusive this morning. Peggy Harlow, the receptionist, told Celia he had telephoned to say he would be in late and could she take his first appointment for him. This was unusual as Reggie selected his own appointments very carefully. Celia had sometimes concluded, rather unkindly, that Reggie only accepted patients whose GP's had already come to reasonable conclusions. Reggie would then give a thorough medical check, injecting his own patter into the routine, sympathise and tut-tut and then confirm the GP's diagnosis and vary his suggested treatment only to the extent of making it appear like a new discovery of medical science. Reggie had once been a very good physician, but lately he had become lazy. He had given up his free consultant work at a nearby hospital, which Celia considered was very bad for him. Hospital work invariably kept one on one's toes.

Among others Celia had to deal with the non-fee-paying patients who had been recommended by their GPs for specialist treatment. If there was something which

24

eluded or defeated her, she passed the patient on to Reggie. Then he would be goaded into ferreting into his memory until he recollected someone who had a similar history, and often out of this would emerge a brilliant diagnosis which still made Celia feel breathless with amazement and admiration. But lately these conclusions had been all too few, as though Dr Marquess couldn't be bothered to think.

Celia's first patient, on this morning, had to wait while she dealt with Reggie's. This was a rich, beautifully-dressed, lavender-haired woman who held a snapping little Pomeranian in her arms. The dog wore a gem-studded collar and wheezed almost asthmatically. Thinking of hygiene, Celia asked, 'Do you mind if your dog waits outside, Mrs Whittingham?'

'My dear young woman,' Mrs Whittingham regarded the other offendedly, 'Dr Marquess never requires me to be separated from Fritzie. As I am his patient, and he has already let me down by not keeping our appointment, I think enough damage has been done. What is your name?'

'My name is Derwent, and I'm sure Dr Marquess had been unavoidably detained.'

'Are you? What do you know about my case?'

'I have read your medical history, Mrs Whittingham, and I am fully qualified. I think I understand all about you.'

25

'Then how is it I'm not getting any better?' the other asked plaintively.

Celia, having read the case history, knew that the woman had a goitre. The pink folds of chiffon around her neck probably concealed an ugly swelling. Her eyes also protruded in the familiar way, though the expensive spectacles she wore minimised this. She was agitated, energetic and yet exhausted by her own gland-driven efforts.

'I'm only getting two or three hours' sleep each night,' she now complained, 'and I can't help disturbing poor, darling Fritzie. Can I, pet?'

'Your dog sleeps on your bed?' Celia asked as calmly as she could.

'But of course. Pomeranians are babies, Doctor. They need their mummies with them.'

Celia wondered if this woman had children, and if so had they ever been spoilt as this animal was. She also decided that if all Reggie's patients were like this one he was welcome to them. She read the notes briefly again and saw that Mrs Whittingham resisted the idea of surgical removal of the affected gland.

'May I examine you now, please?'

When the dog was finally persuaded on to his short legs he promptly made a puddle on the expensive carpet. Celia had difficulty remembering the rule that one never lost

26

one's patience with anyone who was ill.

'I'm sure he wanted his walkies,' she said with a quick smile, ringing for Peggy, who would know what to do. When the puddle was mopped up and a pungent smell of disinfectant vied with the late roses someone had sent Reggie, Celia dismissed the dog in the receptionist's charge without more ado and examined Mrs Whittingham thoroughly.

'You should have an operation, Mrs Whittingham,' she finally told her.

'Oh, no. No! No, I can't have an operation. Dr Marquess understands why.'

'I don't, though. Perhaps you will tell me?'

'Well, I couldn't leave Fritzie. He frets. They nearly killed him the one and only time he went into kennels.'

'Is this your only reason for resisting surgical treatment?'

'It's enough, Doctor, whether you think it important or not.'

Celia realised that she had made her attitude rather too plain to this pathetic woman. No matter how wrong the lavishing of human love upon animals might be—wrong in the sense that they were sometimes allowed to become miniature tyrants and subjected to no form of healthy discipline—it was still often a fact that an animal held more sway over its owner than either close friends or relatives. This was obviously such a case, and a woman who was

27

prepared to endure the miseries of exophthalmic goitre rather than seek almost certain relief in the hands of a good surgeon was not to be lightly dismissed as an eccentric.

'I'm sure you love Fritzie very dearly,' the young doctor said in a softer tone, 'but I feel he would put up with the inconvenience of being separated from you for a while if he knew you would be well and strong and happy again in time.'

The woman sighed tremulously.

'I've forgotten what it was like to feel well,' she moaned.

'I'm sure you have. But as normal treatments don't seem to be helping you very much I think the time has come to take the plunge.'

'Fritzie will fret . . .'

'He will for a while, but this is normal and not an insuperable problem. When he goes to the kennels take whatever he normally sleeps on, and also a few of his toys and his own dish. Or, better still, ask a friend to look after him at home so that everything is familiar around him. If you like I'll look in on him and report to you.'

'He—he may forget me . . .' But the woman was weakening, and after a cup of coffee Mrs Whittingham had agreed to see Mr Weddell, the surgeon who usually took over Reggie's patients when physical treatments had failed to have the desired effect on their conditions. They actually parted friends, the appointment made, and Celia went gladly back to her own patient, who had been waiting all this time, wondering whatever Reggie was up to and if he intended to keep their luncheon appointment or not.

Celia began to feel depressed as the morning wore on and the rain started to descend on Harley Street by the bucketful. She always thought Harley Street had a depressing exterior, which was more than adequately compensated for by the lush interiors of most of the houses and offices. Her own consulting room looked out on to the side of the house next door so she could never be distracted by the splendour of the view, and now the dark brick was even darker in the rain, its Virginia creeper dripping. She had seen four patients, which was usual before lunch, and her afternoon would be taken up by making a visit. Her opinion on a case was being sought by a GP in the Harrow district. She had felt quite pleased about this, initially, for it was the first time she had been asked for by name. All the reading and research which she had carried out during these past six months on the diseases and malfunctions of glands, the histories she had memorised and the gleanings from Reggie's store of knowledge of the subject was apparently beginning to pay off.

But before she could enjoy her afternoon she had to meet Reggie and give him her answer. This would be quite an ordeal, for her as for him, and she was beginning to hope that his non-appearance this morning was the portent that he had suffered a change of mind since last evening, which would not offend her one little bit.

Peggy came into the consulting room looking puzzled.

'There's a Dr Frey on the phone, Dr Derwent. He's foreign and I can't quite make him out. He mentioned Dr Marquess . . .'

'I suppose Reggie has his own doctor, too,' Celia mused, never having considered this possibility before. 'Perhaps he isn't well, or something. It's most unlike him not to turn up like this.'

A few minutes later she turned away from the telephone in the office looking stunned and very white. Peggy regarded her with round, dark eyes.

'Dr Marquess is—dead,' Celia heard a stranger speak in her own voice. 'He complained of being unwell this morning but decided to get up to read his mail. His housekeeper found him in a state of collapse a little later and called his doctor. When he arrived it was too late. He has reported the facts to the Coroner, but is convinced that Reggie died of a cerebral haemorrhage. He had a high blood pressure, you know. Mrs

Haygarth asked Dr Frey to telephone us.'

Peggy began to cry after a minute's stunned silence, and Celia felt rather like letting go herself. It was difficult to realise that Reggie Marquess's urbane, charming presence would never again grace these chambers. He could not be called a great character, but was a most charming personality for the loss of which mankind would genuinely be the poorer. Celia, who had discovered she couldn't love him, had always liked him and found him agreeable as both colleague and mentor.

'What will happen here now?' she found herself asking. 'I suppose the practice will be sold?'

She felt ashamed the very next minute, as though the instinct of self-preservation was stronger even than grief, but this was not really the case. She was still fighting for self-control and seeking other less emotional subjects for discussion.

'We'll be told, I expect,' Peggy sniffed. 'I'm sorry I cried, Dr Derwent, but I really can't believe it. Shall I make some more coffee?'

'What a good idea! I shall make my trip to Harrow as planned, Peggy. I feel we should carry on as normally as possible. He would have wanted that. I shall phone through to you in case there's any further news.'

★　　　★　　　★

Apparently things had been happening thick and fast in Harley Street during her absence. When she telephoned Peggy was all agog.

'I phoned Dr Marquess's afternoon appointments as you advised, Dr Derwent, and everybody was very sad. Shortly afterwards the telegrams started coming and—here's another lot, now. Half a tick! Now, where was I? Oh, yes. Can you come back here, Doctor, when you've finished? There's a Professor Grainger turned up to organise things. He would like to see you.'

'A professor, eh? Of medicine, I hope?'

'Oh, yes. He's a doctor. He's very nice.'

'Very well, Peggy. I'll be there as soon as I can make it. Make the old gentleman a nice hot cup of tea, or something.'

'The old . . . ?' Peggy apparently choked for a moment. 'Oh, Doctor, you will have your little joke!'

Celia, who had not been joking, looked thoughtfully at the telephone receiver as she replaced it on its rest.

CHAPTER THREE

The stranger was sitting in Reggie's expensively upholstered swivel-chair, and he was not old; in fact he was quite young with a

32

thick thatch of dark hair; and he was not quite a stranger to Celia, though she could not think why.

'Please sit down,' he said brusquely, his attention still upon documents on Reggie's desk, and she did so, feeling rather like a very raw recruit in the presence of an experienced officer.

'Oh, Dr Derwent!' the man exclaimed as he looked up, saw her and frowned. 'Our meeting is getting to be a habit, isn't it?'

She knew, now, that here was the man who had driven her home from the party the previous evening. She had been so full of Reggie's proposal that she hadn't even bothered to ask his name. A professor at thirty, or even less? He must be brilliant at whatever he was doing.

'I certainly regret our having to meet in such sad circumstances,' she replied diplomatically, and added 'sir,' for good measure.

'So do I. My brother will be missed by his particular intimates.'

'Your brother, sir?' she questioned this statement in surprise. 'You told me last evening you were only "acquainted" with Dr Marquess.'

'Which is a fact. Actually Reggie was my half-brother. We had the same mother. There was also an age gap, among others. We had no desire to live in one another's pockets or

33

get in each other's way. It was a most amicable arrangement.'

From this Celia gathered, rather resentfully, that Professor Grainger disapproved of his half-brother, his friends and his way of life.

'To our muttons,' Alan Grainger said sharply, putting an end to the nonsense of idle conversation with the practice's junior assistant. 'I hear you took it upon yourself to cancel three appointments my brother had made for this afternoon, Dr Derwent?'

'Well, yes. I thought it was for the best. I didn't know . . .'

'As you see, Doctor, I am here. I have been here all afternoon twiddling my thumbs. The three ladies need not have been inconvenienced at all, as it happens.'

Celia felt her hackles rising.

'Profesor Grainger—' she said heatedly.

'Call me Doctor, please. This is not exactly a professional appointment.'

'Well, Dr Grainger, then. I was upset. I had to go out and I didn't know what was happening . . .'

'But I did, Dr Derwent. The whole business was under my control and I am used to being busy. Not only did you cause these appointments to be cancelled unnecessarily, but the news of my brother's death was also released with undue haste. I would have preferred to have had him decently cremated

34

before the winds of gossip blew the news around. Now the crowds will be milling around when we do it.'

'Perhaps he would have liked that, Doctor,' Celia said sharply. 'You've admitted that you were chalk and cheese.'

He looked up at her and then down again.

'I will try to remember that you're probably still upset by today's events, Dr Derwent, and so excuse your tone, which is disrespectful, and your comments, which savour of impertinence.'

Celia flushed, and then the discipline of years returned to her tongue.

'I'm sorry, Doctor, on both counts. Please excuse me. I am upset.'

'Are you in a hurry?' he wanted to know.

'Well, I am, rather.' Already Mrs Fern would be eyeing the clock expectantly, she knew. 'I have commitments at home.'

'Oh, then I won't keep you. We must talk tomorrow. You look after your mother, perhaps? Or is it your father?'

'No.' She was fiddling with the case history of her afternoon's consultation. 'Perhaps you would care to glance at this before it's filed, sir? Actually I have a child waiting for her tea. I'll see you tomorrow, then, sir, and I haven't cancelled these appointments, you'll be relieved to know.'

Her smile caught him looking at her in some surprise. She wondered at this until she remembered her somewhat casual reference to Fiona's existence. She hadn't said it wasn't her child and by now he was probably thinking the worst of her. Well, she hadn't exactly sailed highly in his estimation previously. He had seen fit to criticise her on three counts, and one more or less wouldn't matter. Already it was very clear that the old easy reign was over. Professor Grainger, who would not let one slipshod remark pass unchallenged, would scarcely endure some of the more happy-go-lucky aspects of the practice, where patients came late for appointments and were promptly excused because they were rich patients, or friends, or friends of a friend. It was already obvious that if Professor Grainger stayed in his brother's place there would be changes made, and one of these might well be the junior assistant herself.

★　　★　　★

Her eyes round and very blue, Fiona asked, 'Aunty, are you cross?'

Celia collected her thoughts sharply as she buttoned the child's nightdress and gave her a friendly little pat on the rear.

'No, I'm not cross, darling. Do I look cross?'

'You're not laughing.' Fiona accused quickly. 'You haven't laughed all through my

36

bath-time.'

Celia sighed inwardly. You could scarcely explain to a three-year-old child why you didn't always feel like laughing. The uncertainties and vagaries of day to day life were not always conducive to lightness of heart. She teased Fiona for a minute on her inability to roll her r's, and they both made their own peculiar noises on the subject before they joined in a simple prayer and then the child was left to sleep while Celia returned to the sitting room and her thoughts.

She couldn't help still thinking about Reggie, how last night he had been so full of life and his love for her. Last night she had been so happy, and yet she now knew, to her regret and shame, that it had only been the happiness of relief that Reggie had offered her the security of a platform from which to fight the Wicheters in their claim for the custody of the child, with an equal if not a better chance of success, possession being said to be nine points of the law.

In a way she was glad she had not had the opportunity of telling Reggie the truth, that she was not in love with him and never could be. At least he had died without having to be hurt and humiliated in this respect. He would still have died if she had accepted him, and she was rather sorry that as a final gesture she hadn't given him this happiness.

All this was a reaction from the actual

event, however, and if it was given us to know the moment of someone's death, who knows what clumsy and irresponsible gestures we might be tempted to make!

The facts were that Reggie had been consumed by a passion he was, for once, unable to laugh away for a young woman who couldn't return his ardour. She could not even feel very personally about his sudden demise, not like she had felt about Belle and Les and the orphan thrust into her trembling arms. Already Reggie was the past, and the future, in the person of Dr Grainger, loomed large and rather terrifying, an unknown quantity in a suddenly alien world.

*   *   *

The next few days were rather vague in Celia's recollection. They were composed of a series of impressions and the most commonplace events assumed an air of unreality. She had several interviews with Dr Grainger and tried to ascertain the security of her tenure in the practice now that her patron was gone. He was rather vague about this.

'I really don't know, Dr Derwent, what's going to happen. As executor of his estate I do know my brother left the practice to me, but I have my own work in research, and I am not remotely tempted to exchange that for Harley Street.'

'You don't appear to believe, sir, that Harley Street has any reputation to maintain.'

He gave her one of his slow, assessing stares.

'It is Harley Street's reputation which is hardly furthered by the existence of this practice, Doctor, in its present context. It's nothing more than a glorified coffee-house. Of six patients I have seen only two who merited my attention. The others were simply gross or neurotic women with all the collective symptoms of acute hypochondria. As an intelligent woman you must see it isn't good enough. Reggie had been slipping.'

'Doubtless he had been unwell,' Celia said, weak with wrath and indignation through which the voice of truth told her this arrogant man was right.

'Doubtless,' he agreed. 'He wanted me to come in with him about a year ago when he was feeling some strain. I couldn't see my way to comply, and we would have quarrelled—as partners. I must have time to think about things. The will is being read after the funeral tomorrow. Naturally I expect you to attend.' His voice deepened into embarrassment. 'You must miss my brother very much and I—I feel for you. I don't show these things, but I'm capable of fraternal feelings.'

Another time he decided that as it would be painful to speak of certain things she might

39

prefer her lawyer to be consulted. From this, as she gave the name and telephone number of her solicitor, she gathered that the man was showing a rare delicacy. Reggie had probably left her a small gift, along with the rest of the staff, but she did not particularly want to discuss it with anybody and would not be present when the will was read. On this point she was determined, though she kept quiet about it.

Peggy Harlow, the receptionist, accepted Alan Grainger almost immediately.

'I had thought of leaving and getting another job,' she confided in Celia as they searched together for a case history their senior required, 'but Dr Grainger is so nice. I wouldn't like to let him down. Don't you think he's sweet, Dr Derwent?'

'Sweet?' Celia seized on the word. 'Hardly that, Peggy, though we doubtless see him through different eyes. I don't doubt his efficiency, but I wonder if that's enough in a practice like this? I think he's just a bit too efficient and impersonal for our customers' liking.'

A frigid voice spoke from the open doorway.

'It would be a little more efficient on your part, Doctor, if you could produce case histories when required. One could secure documents from MI5 with greater promptitude!'

40

'Sweet?' Celia inquired again, her eyes blazing, as they followed him out of the room. 'I hate the man!'

'Oh, dear!' fretted Peggy. 'Here's the folder, Doctor. It was under the D's by mistake.'

* * *

The day of the funeral was misty and chill for September, and dahlias and asters hung bedraggled heads in suburban gardens. When the cortège arrived at the crematorium Celia was glad she had not joined it at the late Dr Marquess's house, and she could understand his half-brother's irritation that so many had turned up to watch the last rituals of this popular man. The crowd consisted mostly of women, elegantly dressed in black and dabbing at their eyes with wisps of handkerchiefs which didn't even disturb their mascara.

'Poor darling Reggie!' Celia heard over and over as she followed the crowd into the chapel for the final little homily on the true Christian significance of death. She tried to say a little prayer for Reggie's continued well-being and happiness, though she did also wonder how many of those women were ex-girl-friends of his, and she fancied he must be chuckling, somewhere, to see them all gathered together in one place like this and voicing the same

41

sentiments.

When all was over she sighed in relief. In this one year she had had enough of unexpected death and funerals. She hoped Reggie's soul would excuse her if she now went home and enjoyed a long, hot drink to warm herself through.

'Thanks for coming,' a voice spoke from about a foot above her head.

Turning, she said, 'Of course I came, Dr Grainger. I had to. He—he was good to me.'

Was there the faintest trace of embarrassment about the other? She sensed it rather than saw it.

'You'll be coming back to the house, of course?'

'Oh, no, I'd rather not.'

'I think you should,' he returned rather sharply. 'It might be thought odd, in the circumstances, if you are not present when the will is read.'

She wondered why it should be thought odd that she didn't like the idea of sitting around like a vulture waiting for any pickings which might come her way. She found the thought abhorrent and determined on defiance.

'I can't help what people think,' she said simply. 'I've never been in Dr Marquess's house and see no reason to visit it now for such a purpose. I'll see you on Monday, sir.'

She felt him glaring after her, but she

42

refused to be bullied and badgered into acting against her inclination. As it was Friday, and an unexpected release from work, as the house in Harley Street had been closed up for the day, she went home and took Fiona down to the supermarket to stock up on groceries. When she returned and was putting meat-spread in sandwiches for the child's tea, the telephone rang shrilly. It was Mr Meredith, her solicitor, who spoke quite jubilantly.

'Congratulations, Dr Derwent! I know it was a sad loss for you when Marquess passed away so unexpectedly, but it is some consolation when a loved one remembers . . .'

'Whatever are you talking about?' Celia demanded. 'Are you trying to tell me Reggie left me something in his will?'

'He left you everything, Dr Derwent, apart from a few minor legacies to servants and friends and his practice. He was quite a wealthy man, though one must allow for death duties, of course. You should clear seventy-five thousand, and the house should be worth quite a bit, though the land is only leasehold. He has even provided for the child. She is to get a thousand a year until she marries. What a load that will be off your shoulders!'

Celia said, 'I don't understand. My head's ringing! Why should Reggie leave anything to me?'

'Because you were his promised wife, my dear. Fortunately, when I was contacted regarding your relationship with the deceased, I was able to quote the letter you had written to me saying that you were now in the happy position of being able to give your ward a foster-father, as Dr Marquess had asked you to marry him. I am so very happy for you. I know money isn't everything, but it does help to smooth one's way.'

'There's a mistake,' Celia said weakly. 'A horrible mistake. After writing to you I changed my mind. I wasn't going to marry Reggie after all.'

'So what?' the lawyer asked easily. 'You changed your mind once, you would have changed it again. That's the way these things go.'

'No. I would never have married Reggie in a hundred years. I had quite finished changing my mind.'

'You can't be sure of that, Doctor. Surely—'

Celia became almost petulant. For one thing she was shaken, shocked and felt physically faint, not at all in a mood to argue the matter. Something within her, which was inherently Celia and as honest as the day, was protesting vociferously against accepting anything under false pretences, let alone a

44

fortune.

'You're to undo this thing immediately, do you hear?' she said somewhat hysterically. 'I don't want a penny of it—'

'My word, we did change our mind,' Mr Meredith said soothingly. 'You do realise that the child will suffer, too?'

'How can she suffer or be deprived of what she never had? In any case I was not Dr Marquess's promised anything, and you wouldn't advise me to perpetrate a fraud, I'm sure.'

The legal mind took the point immediately and promised to do all that was possible, with the result that early next morning Celia was advised to hold herself available to receive visitors at eleven a.m.

Meredith arrived first, pink face glowing and pale eyes twinkling through pince-nez.

'Dr Grainger and the deceased's representative will be along any minute. They considered it might be more convenient to see you here as you have the child to care for. I explained you have no help with her at weekends.'

'That was very thoughtful of you,' Celia said gratefully. 'I'll look at the coffee, if you don't mind.' When she returned she continued, 'I'm sorry if I was rude to you yesterday. I've had a lot on my mind lately, what with one thing and another, and your news was the limit.'

'Naturally I presumed it was agreeable news, Dr Derwent.'

'It would have been had it been justified, but on that day I delivered the letter I later knew I couldn't go through with a marriage of pure convenience. I tried to fall in love with Reggie, but it didn't work.'

'Sometimes the falling in love comes afterwards.'

'Not with me, because I would never embark on such a venture without the confidence of being fully emotionally accoutred.'

'You're a very strong-minded young woman and I admire you for it. But what a pity!'

The musical chimes of the doorbell made her start somewhat. The thought of seeing Alan Grainger on her own ground made her feel unaccountably nervous. Of Reggie's lawyer she was not nervous at all. The housewife in her made her look round at the flat as she went to answer the door. It was really quite a nice flat with one large sitting room, pleasantly furnished, and two bedrooms. The hall had been recently decorated in white and gold with a fitted rust-coloured carpet.

Fiona was still playing with her doll's house in her bedroom, and as the two newcomers were admitted she could be heard shouting, 'London Bridge is all fall down,' and then

46

there was a crash as toy bricks fell in all directions. Alan Grainger glanced immediately down the hall in the direction of the persistent young voice, and Celia gained an immediate impression that he liked children and felt oddly pleased with the idea. It humanised him in her eyes and added a few points to his credit score. He was rather heavy on the debit side up to now.

She scarcely knew what was about to happen as she served coffee and waited for the lawyers to confer, but it appeared that she was to be given a private reading of Reggie's will. In a nutshell there were two wills in existence. The second one, drawn up the day before his death, was the one which was heavily in her favour. The other was a much more general document in which she wasn't even mentioned. In this the residue of the estate was to be used to found and staff a ward in any hospital, to be named by the executors, prepared to carry the Marquess name down to posterity. Reggie had not been, by nature, a modest man, and this was typical. The new will depended for its execution upon a letter which was to be opened on Reggie's death. This had been duly opened by the executors, and was now read to Celia.

'. . . in the event of Dr Celia Derwent having become my promised wife, or wife, she will be adequately provided for as stated in the later testament, which will then revoke all earlier testaments. I also wish the child Fiona Derwent to be considered as my dependant, in these circumstances, and provided for as stated.'

Celia wanted to cry. She felt her eyes blur and was immediately ashamed.

'I understood there was such an engagement to marry between you and Dr Marquess?' the elderly lawyer, Mr Wainscot, inquired. 'There doesn't have to be a ring, you know, my dear.'

'Dr Marquess did ask me to marry him,' Celia said simply, 'and I considered it because I suppose I was flattered and it would have been nice to lean on somebody for a change. But I had decided not to accept him. My decision was irrevocable and I was nervous of having to tell Dr Marquess, but he died before I could do so.'

'You're a very honourable young lady,' decided Mr Wainscot.

'I should hope so,' said Celia, not taking this as a compliment as it was intended. 'I would have to be a downright crook to accept money not intended for me.'

CHAPTER FOUR

Both lawyers had departed, but somehow Alan Grainger lingered on, so that Celia felt bound to suggest he might like to stay for lunch. She hoped he would take this as a hint that it was time to leave, as she only intended having a small chop for her own lunch and had cooked some mince with vegetables for Fiona, but he accepted with some alacrity and she had immediately to revise the bill of fare and rush to the kitchen to examine the state of the larder, leaving him playing pat-a-cake with Fiona.

She had no illusions but that the child was the magnet which was holding him. He had managed to carry on a conversation with his hostess while being regaled with the contents of the toy cupboard; he had crawled on his knees to retrieve beads and bricks from under the furniture and had drunk copiously of the picture of a small girl wielding a paintbrush with dubious success, her tongue protruding and wiggling with the brush's movements.

'She's a very attractive child,' he had commented. 'One day she'll be a beauty.'

'You think so?' Celia asked in pleased surprise. Fiona's straight hair was cut pudding-basin fashion and she was a very ordinary, lovable little girl as far as her aunt could see. She was also extremely small in every way.

'Wonderful bone structure,' Alan Grainger nodded. 'Those cheekbones! She'll be a smasher.'

Celia found a tin of ham, half a lettuce and a bag of tomatoes. She had bought a melon the previous day and decided this would be preferable to soup as a preliminary. The day was fine and quite warm, a true salad day, in fact.

Half an hour later they sat down at an attractively laid table with Fiona at her own chair-table near the open french window overlooking an area of shrubs at the back of the house.

'This is all very nice and unexpected, Dr Derwent,' her guest said with a deep sigh. 'I live in digs and I usually eat out. You're very comfortable here.'

'But why don't you have your own place with a housekeeper as your brother did? I'm sure that's a much more satisfactory arrangement.'

'I agree. But I'm not so well lined as my brother was, neither had I his capacity for making money. I'm not in the poor-house, exactly, but I hadn't a rich father. Not that I regretted that, for he was a very good and wise one.'

'He's dead, then?'

'Yes. He was an overworked GP and was

still going out on night calls with a raging bronchiectasis which eventually finished him. Mother is still alive, though. She couldn't attend the funeral as she is just getting over a bad fall.'

Feeling that she had rather forced these confidences from him and that it was time to call a halt, Celia pressed more salad upon him and then brought in sherry trifle frothed with cream.

'I have to talk to you about the future,' he said as he enjoyed his second helping of this latter delicacy. 'You have been concerned about your own standing, quite naturally. Shall we discuss it here and now or would you prefer it to be done in Harley Street?'

'Oh, now will be fine,' Celia said, as she swept the dishes on to a tray and took them out, reappearing a moment later with coffee and a glass of milk and an apple for Fiona. Her heart had taken a dip of apprehension, but it was no good putting off the evil day, if evil it was to be.

'I've wondered about the content of my brother's second will, as it referred almost entirely to you and the child. I didn't read the letter, of course, until after his death. I had thought, perhaps, that he and you—er—that you—' he stopped in confusion, glanced at Fiona and then gave her a helpless glance almost scalding himself with the coffee.

'You thought the child might be his?' Celia

helped him, and smiled wryly. 'If I had known of the existence of such a document I would have been terribly embarrassed. I'm glad I didn't. Reggie—I beg your pardon—Dr Marquess knew all about Fiona from the start. That's why he gave me the job with him. I think he would really have preferred a young man, as his patients are almost exclusively female, but I hope I proved myself, eventually.'

'I'm sure you did. You were surprised by his proposal of marriage? You hadn't suspected—?'

'Not a thing. When it happened I immediately thought of Fiona, how she would have a father and his protection. I managed not to think of myself at all until later next morning, when I knew I couldn't go through with it. The rest you know.'

'Who is Fiona's father? Do you never see him now?'

She thought over the questions before she realised the full significance of them. Her face flooded scarlet and she almost choked.

'All this time have you been thinking Fiona was my child?' she demanded.

'I thought—I hardly believed—I didn't know, did I, Dr Derwent? My brother may have been in your confidence, but I am not. There was reference to a child who bears your own name of Derwent. I—I'm sorry if I've offended you. What can I say? I drew a wrong

52

conclusion. Oh, dear—'

'That's quite all right,' Celia said with dignity. 'The facts available to you did rather point the way of your conclusions. Actually Fiona is my younger brother's child. He was killed with his wife in a car smash early this year, and I took Fiona.'

'Car smash,' Fiona said, round-eyed.

'Oh, dear!' said Celia. 'Little pitchers. She doesn't know what really happened.'

'Surely she doesn't understand?' asked Alan Grainger.

'She's a very intelligent child, but I've always told her they are away—her parents.'

'I had a car-smash,' the child said clearly. 'I hurted my head.'

'I didn't even know she remembered that,' said Celia. 'I'm learning more about children every day. Far more that I learned in medical school. I hope you don't feel cheated,' she proceeded with a toss of the head, 'that you came here thinking you might be a sort of uncle to Fiona?'

'Are you my uncle?' the little girl came over to ask. 'I like you. You're nice.'

'Go to your room now, pet,' urged Celia. 'Have your nap and then we'll go to the park.'

Fiona ran off and Alan Grainger rose to his feet.

'I suppose I asked for that, Dr Derwent, but I didn't come here with any claim to the child. It simply didn't occur to me. I just

53

happen to like children. Anybody's children. If you were worried about your job you needn't be, for the next six months at least. I am carrying on in my brother's place for that time. When the practice changes hands it has to be to the right person and these things can't be hurried, so I have secured leave of absence from my university appointment.'

'You'll miss it,' Celia told him. 'I didn't mean to offend you, sir,' she added in a softer tone. 'It was good of you to come here as you did.'

'No, it was good of you to speak up about the will. Everybody but you was satisfied you had every right to a great deal of money.'

'No amount of money can make up for the loss of one's self-respect, Dr Grainger.'

'Now that I know you a little better I can appreciate your view in that regard. Well, Dr Derwent, thanks for the lunch and a borrowed hour with your dear little niece. You will never know what it meant to me. May I say goodbye to her, or will I disturb her?'

'I'm sure the monkey will simply be lying with her eyes screwed shut,' Celia declared, leading the way to Fiona's room. 'She tries to fool me because I insist on a nap before we go out in the afternoon. There! You see?'

Fiona's mouth was quirking with laughter, but her eyes were tightly shut as she lay on top of the bedclothes.

'I'm weally fast asleep,' she declared. 'I'm having a lovely dweam.'

Alan Grainger said goodbye, looking round the small bedroom with a kind of hunger in his eyes and then left the flat without even a backward glance at the figure standing in the doorway watching his departure.

'What a funny man!' thought Celia. 'If he's so fond of children he should get married and have a family. With looks like his I'm sure he shouldn't have any trouble finding a wife.'

But Celia had discovered for herself that it took more than good looks or a proposal to make a marriage. Some people might make a go of things on less than true and perfect love, but she knew that she couldn't and she fancied Alan Grainger was another with similar scruples.

'All that time he was thinking of me as a sort of fallen woman,' she thought wryly. 'Les would laugh about that if he knew. It would have tickled his sense of humour.'

With a philosophical shrug she hauled Fiona off to the bathroom and then dressed her for out of doors. In the park, being Saturday, there were many young couples and their children, many of them so obviously still in love. Celia sighed and felt very lonely for a few awful minutes.

'Now snap out of it,' she advised herself. 'I wonder what brought that on? I have a good job and a dear little girl. What more could any woman want?'

She knew the answer, but she didn't choose to acknowledge it because it was too unsettling. In any case, it either happened to one or it didn't, and at twenty-five a young woman becomes discouraged very easily.

★   ★   ★

If Celia fancied that her new boss had thawed towards her because of his Saturday visit, then she was quickly proved wrong on Monday morning. Unlike Reggie had been, he was several different people at different times, and when he was in his working mood he really saw to it that nobody else had a moment's relaxation. If Celia was 'not busy' then he would require her attendance while he examined his patients.

'One can always pick something up,' he opined, 'and if you're working for your Membership you need all you can scoop up. Exclusive practice is not the ideal teaching medium for a young doctor. Usually it's too specialised. However, we're now opening it up a little.'

Celia felt a little startled at that reference to taking her Membership. She hadn't really thought about bettering her degree since she had taken Fiona under her wing. Now the idea excited and intrigued her. Of course there was no reason why she should not improve herself if this man was prepared to encourage her in such a venture. So long as there was time to cram and write her notes.

It was an eye-opener to an unmarried person just how much work one small child entailed and how demanding that tiny person could be on occasion.

Also Dr Grainger was right when he said the practice was opening up in other directions. Reggie's speciality had been glands, especially as they affected women when they malfunctioned or failed altogether. Now there were still some of these patients coming, and Celia found herself asked to give her opinions on them to her senior, who was prepared to accept the fact that she had gleaned valuable knowledge in working with his half-brother. But there were many more physical examinations than before. Businessmen made appointments for health checks, encouraged by their insurance companies, and one well-known insurance company booked Dr Grainger's services to examine thoroughly all their would-be clients who wished either to increase the benefits of their present policies or take out new endowments.

The variation of work pleased Celia. She discovered that many aspects of medicine were quickly becoming rusty with her, as she evidenced one day when she was asked to examine an asthmatic child, accompanied by his mother. The little boy was pale and undersized for his nine years, but appeared to be quite chirpy and cheeky when he first was admitted to her consulting room. He wandered about touching this and that while his parent ineffectually scolded him. When he picked up Celia's stethoscope, however, the young doctor decided to intervene.

'Put that down, Bobby, please. You can listen to your own chest later when I've finished. Sit down. I have questions to ask first.'

'Haven't you any comics, then?' Bobby demanded.

'I have a picture book. I'm sorry if it's too childish, but we don't get many young people here. There, have a look at that.'

Bobby gave a loud raspberry and dropped the book on to the carpet.

'Wot a place!' he exploded, and wandered towards the french windows. 'Can I go out, Mum?' he asked.

'Not far, now. You got to be examined by the doctor.'

'He seems to be a handful,' Celia observed.

'Yes, well. Poor little soul. When they're always being took bad you do spoil 'em, you know. Bobby's had this asthma now for four years. Will 'e grow out of it, Doctor?'

'We must hope so. There was no apparent distress a moment ago.'

'No, well, that's the way, isn't it? Our doc made this appointment an' I knew 'ow it would be. Right as rain 'e was this morning. There's no saying 'e won't be choking 'isself tonight, though.'

Celia read the doctor's notes the woman had brought with her. She rather wished Alan Grainger had taken this one. Frankly she didn't know what more she could say or do to help Bobby overcome this terrible thing. One might as well tell a nine-year-old boy to relax, when he felt an attack coming on, with equal success if one required him to fly.

She discussed various allergic conditions with his mother. Were there feather pillows on the beds at home? No, these had been exchanged for Terylene ones long ago. Had they a cat? No, pussy had been destroyed after Bobby's second attack. Even fur rugs and collars were not allowed in the house and still the attacks went on, monotonously, so that the boy was missing a great deal of school and still could not read properly.

'Which is why he's such a one for 'is comics,' the mother went on. ''E can't get enough. We spend a pound a week on those alone. The pictures 'e can manage, you see, an' what's written in those little balloons.'

'Then we'd better try to do something, hadn't we?' Celia asked with more confidence than she felt.

There was an interruption as the door opened and Alan Grainger stood revealed with Bobby in tow.

'Your patient, I believe, Dr Derwent?' he asked pleasantly enough. 'He wants to be a doctor and has just been investigating all my accoutrements. Also, I happen to be in the middle of a consultation. Sit down, lad. Read your book.'

Celia tried not to think that she had grown pink with embarrassment and was relieved that the boy's mother was taken up with scolding him once again. He deigned to sigh noisily and open the pages of the book with much rattling of paper.

'Perhaps I should examine him now,' said Celia, without really feeling she was any the wiser for the conversation. She could imagine the child's mother asking her GP, 'Couldn't Bobby see a specialist, Doctor?' and the harassed doctor, overworked and underpaid, would finally capitulate and say, 'Very well, Mrs Parrish, I'll see what I can do,' knowing full well that as long as a patient believes something is being done for him, something may well be done by the sheer act of faith. But small boys are not exactly attuned to faith. They only believe in results, and Celia was dubious of her own ability to achieve results in relieving Bobby's condition. She hadn't even seen him having an attack, which might have helped, though she doubted it.

At that moment, as though sensing her predicament, Bobby obligingly drew a long breath which whistled like a kettle through his chest. He dropped the book he had been looking at, open at a page of nursery rhyme pictures and gazed at his mother with eyes which were almost starting from their sockets.

'There, lovey,' crooned Mrs Parrish, glancing at the young doctor almost triumphantly. 'We was counting our chickens too soon, wasn't we? He's off, and Gawd knows when he'll finish. An' I didn't bring his pills with me, bless 'im. You'd better give 'im something, Doctor, quick!'

CHAPTER FIVE

For a moment Celia felt a panic welling up within her bosom. Asthma—asthma—what did one give a child for an attack of asthma? Already she appeared to have been removed from the general atmosphere of medicine embraced by a large hospital for years, instead of a mere six months. She had grown top-heavy in her knowledge of the glandular system to the exclusion of almost everything else; the sex glands, the growth glands, the pigment glands, even the mysterious thyroid, she now knew quite intimately, but a small boy with eyes popping out of his head in near-suffocation as he struggled for breath, his bronchial tubes temporarily restricted and wheezing and rattling like the inside of a very old bus, had her baffled.

'Stop and think!' she bade herself sternly. The mother had already loosened the child's shirt-collar and was wiping an ooze of spittle from the corner of his gasping mouth.

'Doctor's getting something for you, darling,' she said calmly, much more calmly than Celia felt capable of handling the situation. She remembered the next minute a valuable rule, however. Whatever is constricted must be expanded, artificially if necessary. Adrenalin was a great expander; it enlarged human hearts to allow them to take on greater responsibilities and it opened up tight chests. Why had she momentarily forgotten this?

'Because I'm forgetting too darned much, lately,' she told herself grimly as she drew up three minims of the drug into a syringe and reminded herself that only one minim per minute must be administered intramuscularly.

Bobby glanced at her as the needle plunged into his arm, but he was by now so blue and troubled that he couldn't have cared less how many needles were shoved into him. His whole being was shaking and shuddering in the act of fighting for breath; his heart was labouring and the pulse ran like water under the transparent skin of the wrist.

While two minutes passed Celia headed a

treatment card with Bobby's name, the name of his GP and the date, then she filled in various hieroglyphics which would make sense only to another doctor. These were details of the child's past history, his present attack together with his blood-pressure, which she had remembered to take before treatment, and then details of the drug, its dosage and the time administered.

There was little improvement after the first injection, so she administered a second, saying a little prayer as she did so. Did Bobby's cough become a little more loose, his cheeks lose a little of that blueness?

The third minim brought a decided measure of success. Bobby finally got his breath sufficiently to wail, 'Mum, that was a bad 'un!'

'I know, lovey,' Mrs Parrish looked helplessly up at the young doctor. 'It's not right, is it?' she demanded. 'I mean it's not right a young child should suffer like this? Any young child—from anything. You've got to 'elp 'im, please, Doctor.'

Celia had the grace to feel ashamed. What was she doing here in Harley Street, taking over a patient whose own GP had come to the end of his tether, when she hadn't even been able to remember the recognised treatment for an asthmatic attack without raking back through her mind like an old filing cabinet? She desperately wanted to be able to help

Bobby, not only to relieve this present attack. Somewhere along the line there was a cause—a *cause*—but whether the attacks were triggered off by a nervous, psychic or physical reaction she simply couldn't begin to think.

'Do Bobby's attacks always come on as suddenly as this one?' she asked the mother, playing for time.

'Yes. He'll be reading his comic, happy as a sandboy, and bingo! Of course his pills do 'elp, but a life of pills, I ask you!'

'Some children suddenly grow out of it,' Celia told the mother.

'Yes, I know.' Mrs Parrish's tone implied she hadn't come to Harley Street to be told this. Until Bobby did grow out of it, should he be one of the lucky ones, there were sleepless nights and worrying days to be endured.

Bobby was sitting up on the examination couch and was once again reading the picture book. His lips awkwardly framed the words of the nursery rhyme; obviously he was very backward for his age. Apart from the fact that his breath left his lungs like a whistling kettle he was now no longer in distress. He pounced triumphantly on a page in full colour, examined it in detail and then piped, 'Mum!' in a tone of desperation and once again began to fight for breath and—apparently—life.

'I'm going to consult Dr Grainger,' Celia said promptly, picking up the house phone.

'I'm sure he'll want to know about Bobby.'

'Having trouble?' Alan Grainger's voice came cool and clipped in her ear.

'Yes. Two attacks in fifteen minutes. Very severe. The child is quite blue. I—I would be glad if you would look at him.'

'What have you done about it?'

'I've injected three minims of adrenalin over nine minutes. It seemed to work, then it started all over again.' She lowered her voice. She couldn't be heard in any case for the noise of Bobby's laboured breathing. 'His mother knows more about him than I do. I'm sorry to have to trouble you.'

'No trouble. I used to specialise in the respiratory system before I took up research. I shall be a few minutes. Try a tablet of Isoprenaline; you'll find some in the cupboard. Better make it half and we'll repeat in half an hour if necesary. Get all the gen you can and keep the laddie quiet, even when he comes round a bit. OK?'

'Thank you, sir.'

The Isoprenaline, which had not been in use in her hospital, that she knew of, brought the attack to a welcome close, and Bobby breathed without even a whistle. He was tired, however, and went to sleep on the examination couch without more ado.

While they were waiting for the senior practitioner Celia read her notes on the case. 'Attacks come on suddenly, while reading his comic.' She decided that there was no need to mention the comic. It looked rather foolish and unprofessional and she had doodled it in out of sheer nervousness. She drew a line through the phrase and continued to question Mrs Parrish. When Alan Grainger entered the room she sighed in relief and willingly handed over.

She was somewhat reassured that he asked the mother similar questions to the ones she had asked, and referred to her clinical notes, only finding it necessary to add a word or two here and there. He then woke Bobby up, cracked a joke with him and began a thorough physical examination.

'Well,' he concluded, 'the Isoprenaline appears to bring relief. I'll give you a supply of the tablets for the immediate future and notify your doctor, Mrs Parrish. I see Bobby has been taking Ephedrine, but we'll give that a rest for a bit.'

'And there's no 'ope, Doctor?'

'There's always hope, my dear. I'm going to read Bobby's history—his case notes, that is—at leisure. If necessary we'll see Bobby again in a month.'

When the couple had gone Celia asked, 'Is there really anything to be done about the child, sir? It's so very distressing to see—'

'He has been sent to us as the Scotland Yard of the business. We have to find the criminal responsible for bringing on the

66

attacks. As he is your patient, Dr Derwent, I suggest you do some detective work. Come to me for the criminal file before you leave.'

At the time Celia didn't profess to understand him. She was a little resentful when, at four-thirty, he handed her a mighty tome entitled 'Disorders of the Respiratory Tract.'

'Asthma is covered between pages one hundred and seven and one ninety-three,' he told her kindly. 'You'll find it as fascinating as a whodunit, I'm sure.'

'He needn't be so blooming patronising,' she thought unkindly, as she waited for the Jaguar to get out of the way of her own car. 'Just because I don't know a lot about asthma, it doesn't mean that I'm a complete failure in my job.'

Yet she nourished a feeling of guilt that Bobby had found her inadequate, and the sensation was unpalatable. She shouldn't be in a job like this. She should still be working in a hospital or tagging on with a firm of GPs and gleaning all she could about everything under the sun.

Circumstances had forced her hand, but that was no reason why she should cease to further her general medical knowledge in her own time. She should not resent having to read up about a subject which had found her wanting; she should be glad of the opportunity to acquire knowledge.

Once Fiona was in bed she resolutely opened the great book and turned to the noted pages, beginning to read at first through stifled yawns and then with a deepening of concentration as the evening wore on. It began to come back, all that she had once been taught on the subject, and she learned a great deal more.

How many occupations could aggravate the human chest sufficiently to bring on asthmatic attacks! There was cigarette cutting, cotton carding, stripping and weaving, poultry plucking and cotton picking and threshing, all of which irritated membranes in the chest, not to mention the more obvious causes such as mining and allergic influences.

But all this more or less applied to industry, and young Bobby was not yet among the wage-earners of the world. She must keep on reading and hope to find something which applied to his particular case.

She came upon another occupation which merited a whole paragraph. Apparently there were printers suffering asthmatic attacks who were allergic to inhaled acacia, or gum arabic mixed with isopropyl alcohol used in colour printing.

A light appeared to flash out a signal in Celia's mind. She read the paragraph again, not daring to hope. Colour printing, or at least some colour printing, evoked in her mind that delicious odour given off by brand-new books which so intrigues us when we are children. Brand-new comics have the same odour. Bobby read scores of comics because pictures conveyed more to him than words; he had suffered two attacks in the consulting room while poring over a new book of rhymes she had herself placed for the benefit of any child patients from the top-heavy store she had for Fiona's delectation. It might well be that the fumes from the colour-printing sprays were the allergy responsible for Bobby's asthma.

She was so excited that she wrote up everything she had read on the subject, adding her own comments and placing the sheets in Bobby's file, which she had brought home with her. She could scarcely wait for the morning to show the notes to Alan Grainger, hoping for his confirmation and possible praise.

He read them over gravely when this moment at last arrived and at first didn't speak.

'You don't think it could be—sir?' she asked, her disappointment patent.

'I think it is, Dr Derwent. Your detective work may have been well worthwhile. Would you care to dictate the letter to the child's doctor, suggesting that Bobby's literature is vetted from now on? He'll have to go more often to the pictures, of course, to make up for it, and he's going to have something to say about it himself. But I think if it's put in Mama's hands she'll handle him. Well done!'

Celia went to dictate the letter feeling like a superwoman and very happy. She was packing up the file to return it to the GP when she discovered the rough notes she had made yesterday on the case with the remark about the comics crossed out. Over this, written in red ink, Alan Grainger had put, 'Possible cause gum arabic? Two cases Marley Children's Ward.'

'So he knew all the time!' she exclaimed, slamming the file shut. 'Why didn't he tell me? Why did he have to set me to work on all that literature after a hard day's work?'

Her elation had gone. He had simply turned her loose with all the clues hoping that she might spot the right one. If she didn't, well, he had the matter well in hand.

'He must think I'm a child,' she grumbled fiercely, 'who has to have the credit because it might encourage me. Well, I'll cancel the letter and dictate another giving credit where it's due. I feel a complete and utter fool. Why did I have to rush in to him asking for a pat on the head like that? I might have known he was leading me on. After all, he's not a professor for nothing.'

★   ★   ★

70

When they had been working together for a little over a month an innovation was introduced into the practice; Alan Grainger hired a nurse. In Reggie Marquess's time a nurse had not been necessary. Most of the patients were mobile and rarely required to undress, and if they were then Celia had been asked to step inside and chaperone. Peggy had been there to take notes, if required, but she had no nursing experience, though she had acquired a genius for deciphering the hieroglyphics of the doctors' writing which she transcribed into typescript.

Peggy didn't seem to resent the new nurse at all; she welcomed her as someone to gossip to at odd moments and she was by now inclined to believe that Dr Grainger could do no wrong. If he wanted a nurse then he must have one. Celia was not awfully enthusiastic over the newcomer once she saw Nurse Romilly and Dr Grainger fall on one another's necks as old chums. It appeared that they had once worked together at the same hospital, and this must have been a telling time in both their careers as they seemed to do a good bit of reminiscing together with tales about 'old Harrison' and 'Sergeant-Major Mooney,' the RSO and senior midwife of their common hospital.

Celia regarded this intimacy with some resentment, in that she was temporarily left out of the conversation. She also could see—with only half an eye—that Isa Romilly was breathtakingly lovely with her silver-blonde hair and china-blue eyes, and seen through the eyes of the unattached male must appear very desirable indeed. In fact Celia was prepared to dislike the newcomer on sight, and must have shown her hackles on more than one occasion, for Nurse Romilly avoided both her and her patients as far as humanly possible.

One day she appeared escorting a young girl who was having a weight problem and had been sent by her doctor for examination and advice.

'Dr Grainger says he can spare me, Dr Derwent, if you would like me to stay,' Nurse Romilly said guardedly.

'That's quite all right, Nurse,' Celia said coolly and crisply. 'We won't need you. Janet and I are going to talk for half an hour or so. I'm sure that would bore you.'

The door closed with the slightest suggestion of a slam and Celia smiled a little grimly and began to talk with her patient.

After a little while the telephone rang on her desk.

'Excuse me, Janet, please.'

It was Alan Grainger.

'Dr Derwent, when can I talk to you?'

'Er—well—what about, sir?'

'About this practice, its personnel and

function. How about lunch at Maxwells, one-fifteen?'

He had never asked her out to lunch before and she felt a little disappointed about having to confess that she had arranged a lunch-time appointment for an out-of-town patient.

'Damn!' he said frankly. 'I have a table for two laid on. Very well, I'll take Isa.'

She was a bit nettled, feeling that Isa had probably been to lunch with him many times.

'I'll see you at two-thirty on the dot in my room,' he told her, and replaced the receiver.

She wondered what the summons was all about, and at half-past two she found out. Alan Grainger was puzzled and annoyed.

'Why don't you get on with Nurse Romilly?' he demanded, just as she was studying his profile and deciding he was really too handsome for words. Caught off guard, she stammered and stuttered a little.

'What do you mean, not get on—er—sir? I have very little to do with her. Surely you don't expect me to take her out to lunch?'

There was a small, shocked silence.

'Now that was bitchy of you, Celia. It came out in a rush. That is exactly your attitude since the girl came.'

She felt an overwhelming of several emotions, not the least an awareness that for the first time this man had addressed her by her Christian name.

'You think I'm jealous of her, or

73

something?' she asked with a light laugh which rang false in her ears.

'Well, are you?'

'How absurd—!' She stopped her protestations because this man was a lie detector with eyes like gimlets. 'I hadn't thought about it,' she said with a sigh, 'but I suppose I am.'

'Why?' His astonishment was decidedly flattering to her ego, somehow. 'What have you to be jealous about? You've got ten times the ability, ten times the job, ten times the—' she awaited with interest what was forthcoming and felt a little disappointed when it was—'advantages.'

'Perhaps,' she said, 'all this quickly boils down to nothing when one has no time to be—a woman.'

'You're overtired, perhaps?' he asked kindly.

'Not overtired, just outfaced by all that's to be done. But that's doctoring, and I went into it with my eyes open. Now that I'm studying again, I do feel rather hemmed in at times, but that's no excuse and I don't offer it as such. Has Nurse Romilly complained about me to you?'

'No. She merely observed that you don't seem to want—or need—her services. I told her you do but are afraid of imposing. Please prove me right. She needs this job. Her husband is an invalid.'

74

'Oh. I didn't know she was married.' Celia warmed to Isa Romilly immediately and felt almost ashamed to admit it.

'If one can call it that,' Alan Grainger said drily. 'He has been in a mental home for four or five years since the wedding. Fortunately there's no child.'

'I—I'm very sorry,' Celia whispered.

'So there's nothing to be jealous of, really, is there?' he asked with a cool little smile.

'No. I see that now. I feel rather small. But there,' she smiled as coolly back at him, 'I suppose that's what you intended, sir.'

'I happened to think Isa has enough on her plate without having you as an antagonist at this end. I knew you were a nice enough person to agree once you were conversant with the facts.'

Celia began to laugh.

'I would dearly like to argue the toss with you, sir, but you make it absolutely impossible. I thought, once, you didn't understand women; now I think you know us only too well.'

Her laughter stopped in mid-air as she met his interested glance. He was approving of her. She felt as though he had patted her kindly on the head and admitted a desire for it to continue. She liked his approval far better than . . . Her thoughts stopped dead with a mental gasp as she realised the truth. She was beginning to look on Alan Grainger as a man rather than a clever doctor and her boss. This was why she had resented Nurse Romilly, because she was so pretty and Dr Grainger apparently enjoyed her company. Perhaps he did like the nurse, and the husband in a mental hospital was an insuperable object to their affections.

She gave him another nervous glance, but he did not appear to be suffering from frustrated love, and she had a rooted conviction that he would never have placed his sweet temptation right here, where it could tantalise him every day, if there was any danger in the situation.

'No, he's heart-free,' she concluded wryly, 'and that includes me, too, so I'd better get back to work and common sense. He'd never see me like that in a thousand years. I must be mad.'

'May I go now, sir?' she asked aloud.

'Certainly, Dr Derwent. But you are not to overwork. Do you hear? How—how is your little charge?'

'Thriving, thank you.'

'Good. We must have that lunch one day when it's possible. Relax a little more when you can. Go out with your boy-friends. After all, every young mother has had these pleasures at one time. You have been landed with the rough end of the stick, but don't forget there is another end to it.'

'Very good, sir.' She didn't want him to go

on and on as though he really knew there were no boy-friends, as though he knew she inwardly felt deprived.

Isa Romilly tapped and entered the room. She stopped uncertainly as she saw Celia rising from her chair.

'I'm sorry, Dr Derwent, I didn't know you were in conference. Don't let me interrupt you. I can come back later.'

'That's quite all right, Nurse,' Celia said quietly. She knew Alan Grainger was waiting for her to make the first conciliatory move, wondering how she would go about it. 'I was just leaving actually. I wonder if you could come in and help me with an old lady in about half an hour? She has a history of cardiac failure and full examination will be a slow business. That is if Dr Grainger doesn't need you . . . ?'

'No, that will be fine,' nodded that gentleman. Celia again received one of those mental pats on the head as she made her exit, and Isa Romilly said rather breathlessly that she would look out for Mrs MacTaggart and bring her into the consulting room as soon as she arrived.

CHAPTER SIX

Celia wanted to think in solitude for a few minutes, and sank thankfully into her own chair, riffling through the papers in Mrs MacTaggart's file desultorily.

'I am definitely attracted by that man,' she told herself, 'so what do I do about it? All unknown to me Reggie fell in love with me, but he was a man and in a good position, so he could declare his feelings. I'm not in a particularly good position and I'm a woman. Also I've taken on the responsibility of a young child. I can't declare my feelings to Alan Grainger, so I'd better overcome them as quickly as possible. I must watch out, whenever I'm alone with him, that nothing shows. I don't want him to feel sorry for me or think I'm a fool. Obviously hundreds of women have been in love with him at one time or another, he's so darned good-looking and attractive. I wonder if ever he cared about anybody, and what happened? Ah, I believe that's the old lady arriving now. A chauffeur-driven Rolls-Royce? That means a pile of money, and she's eighty-six and can't buy a new heart. Ah, well, let's see what we can do to put her on a bit longer. Thank heaven for work!'

For a few days Celia found herself

deliberately looking out for Alan Grainger and drinking up little cameos like a potent wine. She told herself that it was hopeless and stupid and that she must stop it, but, like someone facing a particularly rigorous diet, tomorrow was always a good day to actually start on it.

One morning he came up to her looking quite eager.

'Dr Derwent, I believe we're both free until lunch time?' He knew this, for he arranged all her consultations as well as his own, so she nodded and waited for him to proceed. 'Care to come round to Wimpole Street with me to the Royal Society? There's an exhibition of photographs and X-rays of radio-activity victims. It's a bit gory, but that is my subject, research and so forth, and I believe there's quite a bit of stuff I haven't seen already.' He took her arm, not knowing what this friendy gesture wrought in her for a panic-laden moment. 'Come on. Put your bonnet on. We'll take your car. It's easier to park.'

She 'put her bonnet on,' or rather, her heavy loose camel coat, and brushed her hair to shining softness before sliding into the passenger seat of her small car. Alan Grainger looked enormous behind the wheel where he was quietly sitting examining the controls.

'No heater?' he asked.

'The button came off,' she explained airily.

79

'I have a rug if you're cold.'

He obviously thought she must be joking and laughed.

'If you can stick it I think I can,' he told her. 'I'm a warm-blooded creature.'

'That I wouldn't know,' she said archly, and felt his gimlet gaze upon her for a moment before he pulled out of the narrow alley where the car was parked into the stream of traffic making its way down the world-famous street.

'Actually, I don't know why we're driving at all,' he said after a minute's frustrating progress. 'We'd have done much better on foot. A hundred years from now some bright lad or lass will be doing research on why everybody is atrophied from the waist down, and we already know the answer. It's the damned car.'

'I walk a good deal with Fiona,' Celia said virtuously. 'She hates the car. It makes her sick.'

'Get her to clutch a penny in her hand.'

'What does that do?'

'It gives her an area of concentration and relaxes her tummy. It's simple psychology.'

'If you think simple psychology works with children you'd better not have any,' she retorted.

'Ah, a cynic, and so young!'

'I'm not all that young,' she told him.

'You poor senile, twenty-six-year-old

thing!'

'How did you know that?'

'You had a birthday last Friday. I've seen your documents, you know, Doctor, or may I call you Celia when we're off duty?'

'Certainly, sir,' she said faintly, thus putting him at his ease and letting him know that she knew better than to take liberties with him. She forbore to remind him that he had once addressed her as Celia when they were officially on duty together.

'It's a pretty name. Don't you think you're lucky to possess it?'

'I haven't thought about it. When I was a schoolgirl I wanted to be called Georgiana. I thought "Georgie," as a diminutive, was so sweet.'

He gave her a sidelong glance and chuckled.

'But you're not exactly a "Georgie," are you? You're small and trim and neat and decorative.'

'You make me sound like a silly little hat.'

'But you are a silly little hat at heart, Celia. You can't kid me. You're a serious medico and work hard, I'll grant you that, and a foster-parent, but the silly little hat is always just underneath waiting to be let out. Had you married Reggie you could have been a silly little hat for the rest of your days.'

'I didn't happen to be in love with your brother, so I'll have to continue being a serious little doctor for a bit longer.'

'And that's important, is it, being in love?'

'Well, isn't it? I always thought that was the first step to the altar.'

'So often it's the only one, unfortunately. It's so easy to fall out of love again.' He was negotiating parking the car by a vacant meter, so she didn't interrupt him. 'I think marriage should be an intelligent undertaking with the emotions kept firmly in check until after the ceremony.'

'Doesn't one risk that part never happening?' Celia asked in a thin, nervous voice as she slid, unaided, out of her side of the car, carefully locking the door.

'It's a small risk, being the simplest emotion of all to conjure up. One only requires the situation, as a rule, and in marriage one gets it all laid on.'

'You called me a cynic? I'm beginning to see why you've never married.'

He shot one of those metallic glances at her which was like a physical blow in the eyes.

'But I have been married. If you could call it that.'

She was upset and confused by this admission, feeling she had dragged it from him against his will.

'I'm sorry. It's none of my business. I didn't mean to pry.'

'Don't worry, you didn't. I volunteered the information and now we can forget it. Here we are at our "club." It'll probably be crowded. It always is.'

Celia didn't like to tell him that she had never visited the headquarters of the Royal Society of Medicine before and hoped he wouldn't mind if she tagged on after him. The exhibition was informative but rather ghastly, and she found herself shying away from photographs of the results of exposure to radiation. Alan Grainger was engrossed by it all, but Celia began to feel faintly sick and eventually went to the front door and gulped the raw November air. After about ten minutes he joined her.

'Was it all a bit off-putting?' he asked kindly. 'Well, it's my job to ferret out a preventative. Obviously one can't find a cure.'

She was hungry and hoped he would suggest going to lunch as they walked slowly along the pavement towards the car.

'All that rather brought out the silly little hat in me,' she said apologetically, 'but it's not really clamouring to get out, you know. I need my job more than my job needs me. When I started training my only fear was that something would happen to prevent me finishing it. Now that I've got it I couldn't really live without it. That's the truth, sir. I want other things, of course, what woman doesn't? But they're not vital to my existence.'

'Well,' he sighed, and she knew he was going to suggest lunch when there came a most unexpected interruption.

'Cilly! It can't be—it is!' called a fruity masculine voice, and Celia looked up blankly into a tanned, moustached face which looked as though it had just returned from the West Indies or some other island paradise. She fancied she ought to know that face as a hand pumped her own vigorously, but only one person had ever called her 'Cilly.'

'Tony!' she said rather helplessly. Imagine meeting one's old—in fact one's only— sweetheart after four long years in front of a third party. He took her tone of recognition as an invitation to plant a kiss full on her lips.

'I hope nobody—' Tony looked at Alan Grainger and laughed affectedly—'takes all this amiss, what? I haven't seen this girl for such ages.'

Celia made the introductions quickly, adding, 'And he doesn't take anything amiss, Tony, he's my boss.'

Alan Grainger was smiling in amusement, and she felt angry and humiliated suddenly. Why didn't somebody go away—Tony, preferably—and return at a more convenient time in her drab life? She knew that at any moment Tony was going to ask her to lunch, and then Alan Grainger wouldn't, and already that promised to be a loss.

Sure enough Tony said the very next

moment, 'Couldn't we eat together? All of us, I mean,' he laughed again. 'I have loads to tell you, Cilly.'

'Please excuse me,' said Alan, quickly, 'but I can't join you. Thanks all the same. I'll see to your car, Dr Derwent, and that will leave you free. Don't hurry back.'

He saluted the pair of them and strode off, leaving Celia scarlet with embarrassment and a certain amount of mortification.

'Tony,' she said uncertainly, 'after all this time!'

'Yes,' he tucked her arm familiarly into his and drew her along the pavement so that they were thus as they passed Dr Grainger busily trying to manoeuvre the car into the traffic, 'we did rather get out of touch, didn't we? I haven't got hitched yet, Cilly. Have you?'

'No, I haven't.'

'I tried, once or twice, but baulked. Actually it's rather fun in my lark not being hitched. A bachelor gay and all that sort of thing enhances one's popularity no end. Here's my bus. I say, I haven't got a ticket? Oh, blast! That's because it takes up a meter and a half. These American jobs are just a weeny bit huge, aren't they?'

There were so many fins on the car that Celia privately wondered if it was as much at home in water as on the roads, but forbore to ask.

'What exactly is your lark, Tony?' she

asked as she disappeared into the leopardskin-covered interior of the huge car and with much reversing and sidling he finally got the monster clear and at least got as far as the traffic lights without further incident.

'You'll never guess. I'm in the restorative surgery game. Plastic stuff, you know? We mainly do cosmetic cases. Do you fancy a new proboscis? No, I don't believe we could better the one you've got, Cilly. It's a nice little nose. I used to tell you that, didn't I?'

He was obviously so pleased at remembering this that she smiled encouragingly.

'I distinctly remember you did.'

'Here, we'll have a bite at Marat's and let the commissionaire get rid of the blasted motor somewhere and earn his half-dollar.'

Had Tony's voice always been quite so loud? She felt as though Tony was trying to match the car, blowing himself up larger than life. He was wearing an elegant suit, obviously a Savile Row job, and an overcoat of cavalry cloth, military in style, rather short and man-about-townish.

She still didn't know what she felt emotionally about seeing Tony again. He was really the only man she had ever been terribly in love with, so that losing him had really hurt. Of course, she had been young at the time and perhaps a little over-intense, but

86

memory had preserved something which now obviously couldn't have existed at all, which was a shocking thing to have to admit. Why, Tony was an affected bore and embarrassed his companion continuously. One of the things which had originally attracted her to him was his air of worldliness and sophistication, but now he might have stepped out of a Noel Coward play with his juvenile lead conversation and mannerisms.

The more impersonal she kept the tone of their reminiscence, the more this apparently evoked the personal in him.

'That rugby game with Thomas's, do you remember?' she asked. 'I never saw so many black eyes at one time, even in Casualty.'

'And afterwards I drove you down to Dorking and we climbed the downs in moonlight,' he told her, reaching over for her hand, his tawny eyes warm and significant upon her as a blush drenched her cheeks and throat uncomfortably.

'It's all such a long time ago,' she told him firmly. 'One goes through phases.'

'Is that all it was really, Cilly? I was very keen on you, you know, and then I heard about the Waring fellow. You went out with him.'

'Only once, to a dance. You were taking your finals.'

'I was jealous, Cilly. I always have been. Can't bear to share things, especially my women.'

'But I wasn't one of your women, surely? You never even hinted at an engagement. After all, our careers were important, too.'

'Well, supposing we put the past right behind us, do you think we could start again?'

'How do you mean, start again, Tony?'

'Seeing each other, at least. I'm not promising anything, mind. A bachelor gay, and all that. But as fate has caused our paths to cross again, and you're still damned attractive, Cilly, I don't think we should cock a snook at dear old Kismet. Do you?'

'I think we should enjoy our lunch and call it a day, Tony. Too much water has passed under the bridge.'

'Now that's damned unkind of you,' he sulked. 'I ask your friendship and you turn me down out of hand. You never really cared about me at all, obviously.'

'Are you sure it's friendship you want, Tony?'

His eyes wavered.

'I take it that's all you're prepared to offer, Cilly?'

'One can't just take up where one left off years ago,' she said defensively. 'I'm glad I met you. I've often wondered about you, where you were and what you were doing. It's nice to know that you're apparently so prosperous, the car and—and everything.'

'So let me come and see you at least, Cilly. Have you a place of your own?'

'Yes, I have a flat.'

'I live in a hotel. Very efficient and all that, but not exactly home from home. I would like to sample your cooking, a little home comfort, perhaps?'

She handed over her card, feeling a little uncomfortable as she did so. Meeting Tony here in public was one thing, but tête-à-têtes at home quite another. She would much rather have said goodbye now that she finally realised Tony Crawley meant no more to her than any stranger she might meet on a train.

'Who's that character you were with?' he asked next.

'I told you, he's my boss. Name of Grainger and a Research Fellow at the University. He's standing in for his half-brother, at the moment. Reggie Marquess died suddenly nearly two months ago.'

'Oh, I knew Marquess. He came to us about a couple of years ago and we removed a surplus chin for him.'

Celia was shocked.

'Tony, that's a breach of confidence!'

'Rubbish! You're in the game. I wouldn't go broadcasting it all over town.'

'But you did broadcast it to this restaurant.'

'Cilly, who would know Marquess here?'

89

'You did. Anyway, it's the principle of the thing. I really must be getting back now, Tony. Don't you work in the afternoon?'

'Not this afternoon. Day off. But I'll be damned busy tomorrow. I'm operating.'

'Do you work alone?'

'Not exactly. Linslade and Protheroe are my—er—partners in crime.'

She was impressed. Sir Julian Linslade was in the McIndoe class of restorative surgery.

'You're in good company,' she smiled. 'Don't bother to get up, Tony. I can get a taxi.'

Tony insisted on accompanying her, however, back to Harley Street, and parked the great car right outside Alan Grainger's consulting room window while insisting on a goodbye embrace which was by no means purely friendly.

'After all,' he whispered suggestively, 'when you remember what we used to get up to!'

'Oh, Tony,' she was scarlet with embarrassment, 'I'm not exactly a fallen woman, you know!'

'Hah! Hah!' his fruity laugh rang out. 'You're really very sweet, Cilly, and I'm glad I found you again. I'll give you a tinkle, then, my love, and drop in for a jar of ambrosia. Till then—' The car shot off, looking like something from outer space, and in the hall Nurse Romilly told her that Dr Grainger was

90

seeing her patient as his own appointment had cancelled at the last moment.

Celia felt rather cross as she went to her own room and looked about. The morning had been rather pleasant until Tony had crashed into it and then it had fallen off and become somewhat of a bore. It was a nuisance, too, if Tony insisted on trying to revive something which was as dead as the dodo. Still, she thought defiantly, there must be some compensations in being desired after one had concluded one was past it.

But it was no good, she then thought rather miserably, being pursued by a hundred males if not one of them was the right one.

★   ★   ★

Fiona usually slept like a top, didn't object to being lifted at about eleven to perform on her potty and went straight off to sleep again. Sometimes she didn't even appear to wake up for this ritual, reacting automatically, but at eight o'clock on this evening she was hot and restless and insisted on throwing the bedclothes off every few minutes.

Celia did not doubt but that she was sickening for some childish complaint, but it was too early to say which. So far there was no sign of either spot or rash, but these could develop by morning.

'It's funny,' Celia told herself, 'I've seen

the children in hospital and observed them clinically, as a doctor, but with Fiona I'm a dithering aunt first and foremost and the doctor's left a long way behind. No wonder parents take no notice when we tell them not to worry. They can't help worrying. It's happening to someone who's a part of them.'

Anticipating trouble on the morrow, Celia decided it was only fair to tell Alan Grainger that she might not be able to get to work. So far Fiona had not ailed much at all, but if she was going to run the gamut of most of the childish complaints then one's boss might not care for the inconvenience.

'I'm sorry, sir,' she explained when he was eventually brought to the phone—he was obviously spending this miserable foggy night indoors as was she—and she told him about Fiona.

'Have you called your doctor?'

'Not yet. I think I can cope until morning when there might be something to see. I'll call him then. I'm sure he'd prefer that.'

'You must stay at home and look after the child, of course.'

'Well, thank you. I was wondering about that. You see, the woman I employ to look after Fiona has a small boy. If he isn't incubating whatever Fiona has I'll be surprised. They do everything together. So I may have to cope for a week or so. Perhaps you can get a locum in my place?'

'Oh, don't worry on that account. Your place is with the child. Would you like me to come round?'

She was so astonished she answered with a gulp and an 'Er—er—' which he took for an affirmative.

'Very well. It may be an hour before I'm there, but if there's anything I can do I shall be glad to help.'

She felt immediately excited at the prospect and yet apprehensive. What could he possibly do at that hour of the evening which might be interpreted as being 'help'? He obviously couldn't be asked to darn socks or wash Fiona's smalls through. But as the child was the obvious attraction he could maybe sit by her cot while her guardian did these necessary chores and made a bit of supper for them both.

Earlier than she had expected, the doorbell shrilled, and just when the child had slipped into an uneasy doze. Her disturbed wails filled the flat as Celia hastily smoothed her hair—she had managed to change into a fresh, attractive blue wool dress and do her hair in a French roll for her role as sick-nurse—and flung open the front door.

CHAPTER SEVEN

'Tony!' she exclaimed in utter consternation. 'You didn't telephone to say you were coming,' she added accusingly. 'Do come in for a minute,' she said with a little more grace, realising that it was not a very nice evening out of doors and that her whole attitude was flouting the laws of hospitality.

Tony had obviously already been to a cocktail party. He emanated fumes of alcohol and cachous, the one obviously intended to disguise the other.

'I wasn't far away and decided to pop over,' he explained, leading the way into the living room and looking round with interest. 'This isn't at all bad,' he commented.

'Tony, this isn't very convenient,' she said, rather flusteredly. 'I mean I can't give you a meal or anything. Let's make a proper date for you to come over.'

At that moment Fiona wailed afresh for comfort and attention, and Tony stiffened.

'What the hell?' he enquired. 'Was I standing on the cat's tail?'

'That,' Celia said rather sharply, 'is a child, and she's not feeling well. I'm expecting the doctor to call and see her.'

She marched into the small bedroom and made little clucking noises of sympathy which were now coming naturally to her. She gave Fiona a quick cuddle, turned over the single hard pillow, so that it was cool to the hot little head, and tucked the child up again.

'Well!' Tony's voice came meaningly from the doorway. 'So what's this, then? Is that your kid, Cilly?'

'Yes and no. I'm not her physical mother, but I am her aunt and guardian at present.'

Fiona opened weary eyes to demand, 'Who's dat man, Aunty Celia?'

'He's an old friend of mine, darling.'

'I don't think he's old an' I don't like him. Send him away.'

'I love you, too, sweetheart,' Tony said huffily, and allowed Celia to hustle him out and close the door. 'What a little monster,' he decided. 'That's the sort of kid who grows up shouting, "Oo, look at that lady's funny hat!" every time you take her out.'

'Oh, no, she isn't,' Celia said firmly, 'I'll see to that. You mustn't mind her saying she doesn't like you, Tony. She wouldn't like anybody today. She's sickening for something.'

'Good lord! I hope it isn't catching. I would hate German measles at my time of life.'

'Well, I don't know yet. There's no rash showing. Perhaps you had better go. It's all rather distracting.'

'I will push off if you don't mind, old thing. I should get rid of that load of responsibility as soon as possible if I were you. It's most off-putting to your admirers. I'm afraid I can't stand kids. Uncivilised little brutes. Well, so long, Cilly. At least I know where you live . . .' He turned back as she stood with the front door open and regarded her speculatively. 'No meal, no drink, at least send me off with a—' his lips descended and held her imprisoned for a long moment. She tried to think, 'This is Tony kissing me. Why can't I remember the old magic? Why do I just want it to stop and him to go? Why does one grow away from people?'

Then, suddenly, Tony was running down the steps and Alan Grainger was standing there saying 'Good evening,' a quizzical look on his handsome face.

Celia felt guilty as she had on the day Tony had marched her past him arm-in-arm, as though she had been seen playing a part which did not suit her talents.

'I hope I didn't break anything up,' said Dr Grainger. 'I didn't realise you had company.'

'I haven't—that is, I hadn't, when you telephoned, sir. Mr Crawley just happened to be in the vicinity. He's an—an old friend.'

She felt that the manner of her parting from Tony merited this explanation, at least.

Alan Grainger was apparently interested in her affairs, however, for he said rather playfully:

'You know, Dr Derwent—er—Celia, I've

been endeavouring to secure your job in my ex-brother's practice; I've even made it a condition that you be kept on as assistant to a new man who wishes to take it over, but—'

'You're not staying on, then?' she asked in some surprise and shock.

'Not indefinitely. I have six months' leave of absence from my true job, three of which have almost passed, and I wouldn't give that up for anything. But that shouldn't worry you if you really like your work and need it.'

'Of course I need to work. Why do you doubt it?'

'Well, as I was saying, it never occurred to me until now that somebody might want to marry you and take you off.'

Her heart leapt in her chest and then settled down into its normal rhythm once again. He was only fishing, of course, not proposing, so she would play him along a little.

'I'm naturally open to offers, sir,' she said archly. 'Have you had any for me?'

In as light a tone, but with heavy implications he replied, 'I know it's none of my business, but I gained the impression that you can canvass your own womanly charms well enough.'

'Oh,' she returned rather weakly. 'You mean all that business with Tony?'

'I also said it was none of my business unless you're thinking of getting married in the foreseeable future. Dr Wilkes-Mather is quite prepared to take on an assistant with your qualifications and experience; he is in Reggie's line of country, as a matter of fact—wrote a marvellous thesis on the thyroid to take his Fellowship—and I'm sure my brother would be glad to know such an eminent member of our profession would like to carry on the good work. Naturally I don't want to force him—or you—into any contract you may be likely to break for personal reasons.'

'Oh,' Celia said again. 'Well, I'm not intending to marry Tony Crawley, if that's what you want to know.'

They had both settled down in the living room as though Fiona didn't exist. Fortunately she had drifted into an uneasy sleep and was not advertising her presence.

He looked at her without speaking, and she was immediately on the defensive.

'People do kiss and embrace without anticipating marriage, you know,' she enlightened him. 'Mr Crawley and I were once very fond of each other. He wants us to be like that again, or he did before a couple of snags turned up.'

Again he waited politely, so she continued.

'One, I don't want to and two, he doesn't like children.'

'Funny fellow,' he remarked at last.

'So I shall be happy to assist Dr

Wilkes-What's his name.'

'Dr Wilkes-Mather. That is if it all comes off. I thought selling a house was bad enough, but selling a medical practice is worse.'

'I suppose it is when you have all sorts of extras to throw in, such as unwanted assistants.'

'Don't call yourself that,' he said sharply. 'You do very well, I've been pleasantly surprised, I may tell you.'

'Oh, yes? What about young Bobby's asthma? I was floundering and you led me on to arrive at your own conclusions. Don't think I was fooled all of the time.'

'But what is a senior partner for if not to help his junior along occasionally? You'll he happier back among your thyroids and pituitaries.'

'No, really. I've been very happy doing more general work. One does become a bit atrophied working with specialists.'

'It's more and more a world of specialists, Celia, no matter how much one may regret the fact. Why, I heard of a case where a fellow needed urgent surgery in a small country hospital; the anaesthetist had had a coronary only ten minutes earlier and nobody could be found to take over the anaesthetic machine for the operation. Fortunately there was an old RMO on hand who remembered the days of the ether pad, so they at last got started, and the patient survived the old-fashioned techniques.'

Celia smiled.

'Anaesthetic machines do look rather terrifying to the uninitiated,' she agreed.

'So you are not thinking of getting married?' he asked once more, as though they had never deviated from that subject.

'That's asking too much,' she joked. 'I'm always thinking of it. I'm a perfectly normal woman with natural instincts. I think the answer to your question is that I'm not planning marriage in the foreseeable future. I do wish you wouldn't keep on making me say that. I'm beginning to think I'm a failure.'

'Rubbish! You're just extraordinarily selective, as I am myself. The circle of possibilities is extremely narrow, but still existent. If you're not considering marriage—and you did once regard my brother as a possibility, no matter how briefly, and so I interest myself on his behalf—what's going to happen to Fiona?'

'Fiona!' she echoed dully, not understanding him.

'Yes, Fiona. Your solicitor read me extracts of a letter you had written him after Reggie had proposed. At that time you were happy that this afforded you a strong case for keeping the child. I take it that somebody else was claiming her?'

'Yes, her mother's adoptive parents in Australia. Actually I've been trying not to

100

think about that. Nothing more has happened, but if it does come to court I suppose I'll lose her. They can give her everything. Belle's life with the Wicheters, after living in an orphanage, was like a fairy story. But after almost nine months I can't remember what it was like not having a child in the house. I would miss her terribly. I really don't want to think about it.'

She jumped up to busy herself by making a light meal, but, like Nemesis, Alan Grainger's voice followed her into the kitchen.

'You ought to think about it, Celia. Hiding your head in the sand won't alter the facts, and you should be building your defences. You probably have a stronger claim than you think. Mutual love and affection is no mean start.'

'My love for Fiona won't matter two hoots,' she called back, 'and a young child forgets so quickly. She would grow to love the Wicheters; they're good people.'

'Perhaps your youth might stand on the credit side,' he was by now standing in the doorway thoughtfully regarding her. 'These people must be getting on?'

'They were past forty when they adopted Belle, so we may have a point there. Can you think of any more, sir?'

'I was wondering if I could help. If I undertook to back you up in your guardianship, perhaps guaranteeing certain financial ventures such as education and so forth . . . ? Please don't look offended, Celia. My brother—God rest him—has left me a darned sight better off than our relationship ever deserved. I feel guilty about it. If he was prepared to support this child then so am I, damn it!'

'But he happened to be in love with me when he made those provisions,' Celia told him, 'so it wasn't charity. I would have been giving him something in return for his generosity. I can support Fiona adequately given my health and strength, and I'm no weakling, and my brother had already insured himself to cover her education. I have all that tucked away with a Building Society. So—so there!' she concluded, looking very pink and sailing past him with a laden tray of sandwiches, coffee and a frothy-looking gateau.

'Don't be angry with me, Celia,' he begged. 'I only wanted to help.'

'Your brother owed me nothing,' she insisted, her eyes flashing, 'so you have no debts to take over. I wish you would realise that.'

'I said I wanted to help, that's all. No one need don armour against a perfectly natural concern. Let's forget my brother. At the moment you are my assistant and there is this threat hanging over you. Am I supposed to play the Levite and say I don't care? I do care. There may be legal arguments for the rights of these Australians, but I think you and Fiona are good for each other.'

She relented sufficiently to pass him his coffee and hand him the sandwiches.

'Th-thank you,' she said. 'I'm touchy, I suppose, and I was hiding my head in the sand a little. If I could have fallen back in love with Tony it would have been ideal for my case, I suppose. I happen to need a husband rather urgently, or, more truly, a foster-father for Fiona. I should advertise, shouldn't I?'

'I seem to remember you tried thinking that way once before and decided you couldn't do it, even throwing a fortune away to emphasise your point.'

'Yes,' she wryly agreed. 'It makes me so angry, too, to believe they would think me better equipped to care for Fiona if I was married. I'll do everything for her that her parents would have done—probably more. I earn more than Les did.'

'I must disagree, on behalf of my sex, that you can be both parents in one person. Incomes don't enter into it, or all postmen and agricultural labourers would be childless by law. A man in the house contributes his own individual influence, not always benign, I'll grant you.'

'So you really believe Fiona needs a man in her life?'

'I think you both do, frankly. But all needs are not necessarily met. We have to take what we've got and make the most of it. I happen to believe Fiona needs you rather than several thousand acres in Australia and foster-grandparents. She's a city child. Space would probably terrify her. Look how she has adjusted to you!'

'You are comforting me, Dr Grainger, and thank you,' she said sincerely. 'I'm beginning to think I might have a chance in court, if it comes to that.'

It was after eleven before Fiona reminded the pair of the real reason for Dr Grainger's visit. She sat up in her cot scratching her forehead fretfully, but cheered up when she saw the visitor.

'Uncle Alan!' she said clearly. 'I like you.'

'Flattery will get you everywhere,' he told the child, kneeling down and tickling her through the rails. 'You've got a lovely chickenpox spot coming, haven't you?'

'Have I? Weally? What's a chicky-pox pot?'

'On the end of your funny little nose. No, don't let your fingers feel it. It's there, you can believe Uncle Alan. There are a couple on your forehead, too. You'll look lovely by morning.'

'Is it chickenpox?' Celia asked in some relief as they stepped outside again.

'It's going round, and those spots are unmistakable. She'll probably be as right as rain once they're out, but glove her hands at night so she can't scratch. I think a little liquid aspirin should cool her off and settle her for the rest of the night. You can let her own doctor take a look at her tomorrow just for the record. Well, I'd better get back to my own place and get some sleep. Thanks for the contretemps. I really enjoyed it.'

She brushed against him in the hall and jumped away like a startled cat. Touching him had electrified her but not, apparently, him.

'Goodnight, Celia,' he said in his usual off-duty friendly fashion. 'If it's not an intrusion you might keep me informed as to how you go on with the legal side of things, and if I can be of any help don't hesitate to let me know.'

'I won't,' she promised, and allowed herself to relax when he had gone.

She looked at her reflection in the hall mirror. It wasn't a bad face, she decided without vanity. It had been described as heart-shaped, and her skin had always been good. But it didn't seem to do anything to Alan Grainger. There they had been most of the evening, a man and a woman, and sex had not been allowed to make their meeting the more interesting.

'Well, you either feel like that about someone, or you don't,' she decided philosophically, 'and because I've caught the bug it doesn't mean it's infectious, like chickenpox! I do think it's a bit stupid of fate, or whatever arranges these things. The man I've wasted years over, loving and remembering, comes back into my life and I promptly fall in love with somebody else who is really more in love with Fiona than me. I'm the gooseberry he has to suffer to be her "Uncle Alan"! Ah, well, I suppose I'll get over it, and the sooner the better. Now, liquid aspirin, he said, and gloves. Gracious, I am tired, and no wonder, it's nearly midnight.'

CHAPTER EIGHT

When Celia returned to work, after a few days, Christmas was only two weeks away. Having a child made a big difference at this season of the year, she had discovered. There was a mounting air of excitement about each day and all bedtime stories must have a Christmas theme. One day, a little nearer the festival, they were planning to visit the great man himself in one of the large stores, and Fiona was determined to confide in him regarding the respective merits of a new doll or a pram for the one she already had. Celia was waging a battle with herself not to over-indulge her ward. She would have liked to have seen Fiona's face on Christmas morning when she beheld a new doll in a new pram, but one main toy on every special occasion must be the rule by which they lived so that there was no danger of spoiling.

She doodled 'Must get Fiona's shoes repaired' on her blotter and then took herself firmly in hand and decided that any spare half hours she might have could be well employed in reading for the Membership she coveted. She had settled down to reading a chapter of Dermatology, a subject upon which she knew very little, when there was a tap on her door. Thinking that her expected patient had come early she called 'Come in!' and then stared in some surprise, for instead of Mrs Whittingham, the ex-ophthalmic thyroid sufferer, who was now the right side of an operation which had been one hundred per cent successful and beneficial, a very beautiful, tall, dark woman stood smiling quizzically in the doorway. She wore a tailored suit with an air of complete sophistication and draped carelessly around her shoulders was a blue mink stole. Her eyes were so dark they were almost black, which her sleekly dressed hair was. She could have been Spanish or Italian, but her voice was perfectly unaccented pure English as she said,

'Excuse me, but Alan is busy. I wonder if I could chat to you for a few minutes to pass the time?'

'By all means,' Celia said promptly, deciding that anybody who called her boss 'Alan' so familiarly must be a friend rather that a patient. 'Do sit down.'

'Thank you. My name is Raven. Denise Raven.'

'How do you do,' Celia nodded politely.

'How can you bear to work with Alan? He's the most pernickety person I've ever known,' the newcomer proceeded quite pleasantly.

'Oh,' Celia laughed lightly, 'he's not so bad at all, really. He hasn't been particularly pernickety with me.'

'Really? May I smoke? You must be one of his favourites—' Celia smiled again—'because he can be quite ruthless. Ah!' she picked up the picture of Fiona on the desk and examined it. 'Yours?'

'My niece. The child lives with me, though. She was orphaned almost a year ago.'

'The poor little thing! I bet Alan's adopted her. He dotes on children.'

'They do get on rather well together,' Celia agreed. 'Have you any children, Mrs Raven?'

'No, I—er—haven't. I'm not married.'

'Oh, I'm—'

'That's quite all right.' The dark eyes were hard, bright and somehow strangely chilling. 'It's generally assumed at my age that one must be married. I don't know why. Women are very much more independent of the

108

opposite sex these days, and no stigma attaches to bachelors, nor ever has done. I don't know why a bachelor should be thought rather clever and an unmarried woman a failure. Surely you are a feminist too, my dear?'

'Well,' Celia smiled awkwardly, 'I haven't really thought about it. I suppose I'm a coward. I leave causes to others.'

'Naughty of you! We professional women, who have proved our brain-power, should be strong, firm characters too. There's a deeply-rooted conviction afoot that any woman trailing six offspring at her heels must be superior to an unencumbered female scientist. Absolute rubbish! But I mustn't bore you. You are young and possibly under the influence of your lords and masters still. Or perhaps that should be just one?' The well-bowed lips parted in a smile which didn't reach the watchful eyes.

'One is enough at a time,' Celia laughed, wary of giving anything away to a stranger.

'How right you are, but en masse men are much more manageable. I was just going to—'

The door opened and Nurse Romilly stood there.

'Oh, there you are, Dr Raven! Dr Grainger is free now if you would care to go in.'

No sooner had Celia nodded her unexpected visitor away than Isa Romilly was back apologising.

'I'm sorry about that, Dr Derwent. I hope you didn't mind entertaining Dr Raven temporarily?'

'No, I didn't. She was most charming.'

'You know who she really is, of course?'

'No. Should I? Is she famous? . . . infamous?'

Isa grimaced prettily.

'Take your choice. She's the ex-Mrs Grainger.'

'Oh!' Celia rapidly back-tracked over the recent conversation. Had they mentioned Alan Grainger in any but the broadest sense? She thought not—hoped not. 'Why does she call herself Raven, then?' she asked.

'I don't know. It was all over before my time. She's five years his senior, which makes her—um—thirty-seven, about. I don't know what went wrong, but it was annulled. They've always kept in touch, though. At least, she keeps in touch with him. She used to turn up at the hospital and wait until he was free. I don't think she liked me. She had an idea I was going to fill her shoes, but after I married Ken she was as nice as pie. Funnily enough she's a consultant at the hospital where he seems to be stuck, poor darling.'

'Is she a psychiatrist?'

'Yes, and neurologist. She's very clever, I believe. Beauty and brains don't always go together, do they? I think she's one of the most beautiful women I've ever met.'

'It's most generous of you to say that, Isa. You're not so bad yourself.'

'Oh,' the other blushed as she smiled disparagingly, 'compared with Dr Raven I'm colourless. But there's something about her—I don't know what it is—'

'She's encased in ice,' Celia nodded. 'I know that's how she struck me. However, I don't suppose his nibs would care to think of us gossiping about his ex-wife. Do you?'

'No,' Isa smiled again, 'but I thought you'd better know in case you bump into her again.'

'Yes. Thanks for telling me—'

When the nurse had gone Celia found she minded the thought of the ex-Mrs Grainger having become flesh. All that beauty must once have stirred Alan, have melted in his arms and become a part of him. What could have gone wrong between two people, obviously mature and intellectual, that their union had been annulled?

'That word "annulled,"' Celia pondered, 'it's so negative. It means "wiped out" or "made nothing," and yet how can you dismiss a marriage and all that went before as though you were rubbing a wrong answer from a blackboard? You can't annul people, emotions. I wish I knew what had happened between them, and yet I have an idea, knowing how I feel about him, that if I did know I would feel miserable and sick. Ah, this must be my patient. That's what I need. Work!'

★ ★ ★

Celia tried not to spoil things by questioning Alan Grainger's sudden predilection for her company. Twice in one week he had sought it. Of course Fiona was there, too, sitting between them, and it was Christmas and there were children's seasonal entertainments to which he had invited them; a pantomime five days ago and 'Peter Pan' this afternoon. It was the first time Fiona had been taken to live shows; they had discussed the possibility of her being too young to enjoy such things, but she had been completely entranced by everything she had seen and had shown no signs of being either overtired or unduly excited by these events.

'I think I would like to fly, Aunty,' she now whispered as Peter took off on yet another airborne adventure. 'How does he do it?'

'It's magic, darling, and only a few people know magic as strong as that.'

It would have been disillusioning to speak of wires and harnesses and pulleys. Alan Grainger smiled approvingly across at her and she glowed. If he couldn't love her his approval was almost as good, and she basked in it, thinking how other people might imagine they were proud parents with their child sitting between them; well-off parents in the front row of the stalls of this famous theatre.

All too soon it was over and they were being whisked back to Marchmont Road in the old Jaguar.

'Thank you, it was lovely, we did enjoy it,' she told him, as previously, as she fumbled for her door key.

'Fank you, Uncle Alan,' Fiona seconded. 'Are you staying to tea?'

'Of course you're very welcome,' Celia said hastily, torn between wanting more of his company and appearing to hog it.

'No, I can't stay today,' he said with polite regret. 'It's I who should thank you for a most pleasant afternoon. Perhaps, Celia, we could go out to dinner one evening? How about tomorrow?'

'I'm afraid Fiona's a bit young to go out to dinner . . .'

'I thought you said you knew a baby-sitter?'

'Oh, yes. I can ask Eileen if she's free. May I let you know?'

Eileen was not only free but able to oblige and willing. Celia hardly dared believe in her luck. This time Fiona could not be said to be the attraction. On the other hand one could not assume with a man like Alan Grainger that there was any particular attraction about the evening at all. They were two doctors intending to share a dinner table. That was all. Nothing more must be read into the rendezvous than a cordial desire to please someone else. Employers often entertained their employees like this without any great romance flowering because of it.

Celia found the evening most pleasant. There was plenty of laughter, and Alan had a fund of medical jokes with which to entertain her. They dined at Obertelli's and Celia relaxed in the knowledge that she could enjoy herself without having to think whether it was time to take Fiona to the toilet or take her to be washed after some gastronomic treat.

This was the first of several evenings they spent together, and Celia stopped expecting miracles and took what was offered without question. Once Isa was asked along, too, and it turned out to be a very pleasant threesome until Tony Crawley, who was dining at the same club, gatecrashed and flirted so outrageously with Isa that Celia was ashamed for him and suggested he take her home as she had a headache, thus leaving the other two, as she thought, in peace.

'You don't need to be jealous, darling,' Tony said as they descended the stairs to the cloakrooms. 'That pretty fairy isn't half the woman you are.'

'I'm not at all jealous, Tony. You've done as you wanted for the past four years, so I don't expect anything of you now.'

114

'Then how come we're going back to your place?'

'We are not going back to my place, in that sense. You're taking me home, I hope.'

'Oh! You really have a bad head? It's such an obvious excuse I don't believe anybody was taken in.'

'You—you mean Alan Grainger would think I wanted to be with you?'

'Obvious, my love. I was playing dare with the little blonde piece, your nose was out of joint, so you developed a non-existent headache. It's always the one who's being neglected who gets the headache. Funny, isn't it?'

'I think you're the most offensive man I ever met, Tony. You go back to the party and I'll get a cab.'

'Oh, now, honey, don't be like that. I'm merely pointing out that I saw through your game. I came, didn't I? What more do you want?'

'Frankly, at this moment I would like to kill you. You make me so mad!'

While her eyes were blazing Tony stooped and kissed her full on the mouth. She spluttered with rage, stumbled on her high-heeled evening shoes and grabbed hold of him. He took this as a further invitation, and Celia finally pushed him away only to observe Alan Grainger's stiff, tall figure entering the gentleman's cloakroom.

'We're leaving, too,' Isa volunteered, her cheeks dimpling with amusement at what she had witnessed. 'I say, Dr Derwent, your friend is a devil, isn't he?'

'That about sums him up,' Celia said rather shortly, and went out in a very bad humour to get herself a taxi.

For a week or two there were no further dinner invitations forthcoming from Dr Grainger, but Tony called on her to make his peace and was grudgingly forgiven.

'You're so touchy nowadays, Cilly,' he told her ingenuously. 'I've always tried to poke fun at people, but you're so darned serious all the time. You really should loosen up. Get that kid fixed up in a decent Home where she'll have companions, and go about more, like old times.'

'I wouldn't dream of getting rid of "that kid" as you call her. It's wonderful having a child in one's life. You should really try it, Tony.'

'Now that's a most interesting suggestion. I hope it means you're going to be nice to me, Cilly?'

'Being nice' to Tony always meant submitting to his embraces and kisses. These did not appear to signify more to him than that one was not annoyed with him about anything. Celia did not feel at all physically stirred by him these days and he, too, seemed content to kiss and go his way.

116

One day, at the end of February, the blow fell. An official-looking document which came through the post told Celia that the Wicheters intended applying for the custody of Fiona through the courts, followed by legal adoption, unless her aunt was prepared to surrender the child voluntarily. The letter, which came from solicitors acting for the Wicheters, volunteered the information that whereas, at present, the child spent a good deal of her time in the care of strangers, namely eight hours a day, she would have the undivided care of the claimants both night and day if required; that whereas she was being brought up in a city notorious for its smog and grime, the Wicheters could provide her with a sunny climate, healthy outdoor surroundings and every devoted attention.

There was more of it, which all sounded very fine, like a travel brochure tempting visitors, and Celia was very worried. That Hodson man had done his job well; he had spied on her, using her hospitality to do so, and then stabbed her in the back like this. Fiona had been with her for a year now, and she couldn't imagine life without her. Although it was true that she had to employ someone else to care for her most of the time, this was surely no different from a mother placing her child in a nursery while she went to work herself, or an upper class woman employing a nanny.

'Parents simply don't feel thay have to spend every minute with their children,' Celia told herself. 'When they start school, that's separation, isn't it?'

But she found she couldn't glean any comfort from such observations, and she was worried. She had a busy day ahead of her and to add to her troubles she felt she had a cold coming on.

All day she caught only the merest glimpses of Alan Grainger, but for once she was not looking out for him. She felt too miserable and distrait. At half-past-four, as she was writing up the notes of her last patient, the house phone rang on her table and he requested that she call in to see him as soon as she was free.

She duly presented herself, sitting down in the chair usually reserved for patients, and nibbled her nails fretfully while he finished writing.

'Ah, Celia,' he said at last, 'I wonder if you could join me for dinner this evening? Nothing formal. I now have a very nice flat, with a housekeeper in attendance, and this is a sort of housewarming.'

'I'm sorry,' she said abstractedly. 'Not tonight, if you don't mind.'

'Oh.' His voice gave nothing away. 'Perhaps you have a previous engagement?'

'No. I'm not going out tonight.'

She scarcely waited to be dismissed before

118

rising and going towards the door.

'Was there anything else?' she remembered to ask.

'You do realise that I'll be leaving Harley Street in a fortnight?'

'As soon as that? Well, I suppose it won't make much difference to me. I mean Dr Wilkes-Mather will dovetail in and I'll go on much the same. I hope you have a pleasant housewarming. Goodnight!'

He bit his lip when she had gone.

'There won't be a housewarming without you, Celia,' he told the empty room. 'Nobody else was invited. Not that you appear to care one way or the other!' He struck the desk fiercely so that papers flew hither and thither. 'I'll have to play Mahomet,' he decided harshly, 'and come to terms with the mountain.'

⋆ ⋆ ⋆

On the journey home Celia found her powers of concentration were impaired. She felt stuffy and was going hot and cold by turns.

'Trust me,' she groaned as she finally garaged the car with a sigh of thankfulness that there had been no accident due to her terrible driving, 'to get 'flu with all this worry on my mind. Well, I can't afford to be laid up and that's flat.'

When she had given Fiona her bath and

settled her for the night she rang up the doctor who cared for them both and with whom she was quite friendly.

'Listen, John, I've got this forty-eight-hour 'flu. I can't afford to miss my work, so you must give me an injection or something to keep me on my feet. No, I can't stay in bed tomorrow. I want to sweat it out tonight. I'm going to bed now. If I leave the door on the latch can you call in after surgery and give me something?'

She put hot bottles all round herself and settled down in her bed to wait. When she had grown really warm she relaxed and slipped into a doze. She was roused from this by feeling someone's lips upon her own.

'Alan!' she cried out involuntarily, opened her eyes and started, pulling the bedclothes round her neck.

'Tony! How did you get in?'

'Through the door, my love. I rang and nobody answered. I've been here quite ten minutes listening to you snore.'

'I don't—' she began indignantly, then subsided. 'I think I've got this wretched 'flu,' she explained, 'so I probably do snore at the moment. I thought you were afraid of catching things?' she asked accusingly.

'Not at the moment, my love, I've just recovered from the damn thing.'

He sat down on the bed, waited to be repulsed, and when he wasn't, stretched out

120

full length beside her.

'Tony,' she said nervously, 'this is my bedroom. I think you'd better go.'

'My dear, sweet old thing. She fought like a tiger for 'er honour and all that sort of mush! I just like seeing you all weak and womanly with ribbons I can untie at will.'

She slapped his hand sharply, tied up the disordered ribbons which he promptly grabbed again. She felt so little like fighting with him, or even playing one of his stupid games, that she began to cry. He watched her in amazement for a moment and then seized her rather roughly.

'Here, Cilly, I was only fooling. Stop that, now. I can't bear hearing a female howling. You've always been so tough. Have a good blow and dry up, there's a good girl.'

He rocked her gently until her sobs ceased and then he patted her back as though she were a baby.

'Good old Cilly,' he crooned. 'You must be feeling rotten. Let's have a look at you now.'

Her face was blotched with tears and the ribbons of her nightdress loosened, revealed the alabaster swelling of her young breast. Tony gave a queer, hard little sigh and pulled her to him, not the commiserating friend any longer but the hungry lover.

They parted, breathing hard, as a voice spoke from the open doorway.

'I'll come back later if it's no' convenient.'

121

It was a Scots voice, that of Dr John Bute.

Celia glared at Tony, who murmured with a self-conscious grin, 'Sorry, Cilly.'

'It's quite convenient, John,' Celia said clearly, wondering how one did refer to a scene such as had passed, if one referred to it at all. She then saw, with horror, that behind John Bute was the tall figure of Alan Grainger, and she had never seen him looking so angry in all of their acquaintance.

'What's this then?' Tony asked, having recovered himself somewhat. 'A medical conference over a measly little 'flu bug? Can anybody join in?'

'Dr Crawley is just leaving,' Celia said very pointedly.

'Yes, well,' Tony nodded cheerfully all round, 'must get on, I suppose. Be seeing you, Cilly.'

'I'll wait in the next room,' Alan Grainger said heavily.

Celia looked rather wryly at John Bute as he took out his stethoscope and shook up a thermometer.

'Actually that wasn't as bad as it looked, John,' she said awkwardly. 'Tony's just a fool. He found the door open, came in and then ran true to form. It doesn't mean a thing with him.'

'You don't have to explain tae me, Celia.'

'I know I don't. But my boss—!' she grimaced. 'I suppose he saw?'

'I expect so. He was looking. I met him outside and he was most concerned that you had sent for me. Dinna worry about it. Bonnie lassies have that effect on some people. I'd be sneaking a wee cuddle masel' if it wasnae for Mrs Bute!'

CHAPTER NINE

Celia put the two tablets and the anti-influenza serum in a safe place, drew on her warm towelling bathrobe, because she was perspiring, and went heavy-footedly towards the living room to meet her Nemesis.

Alan Grainger rose to meet her. He was no longer angry but flintlike. She did not ask herself why he considered he had any right to be angry with her, no matter how she behaved out of duty hours, she simply knew she was unhappy under the cloud of his displeasure.

'I hope you're feeling a little better?' he opened the batting.

'I'm feeling no worse, thank you,' she returned. 'I'll be all right tomorrow.'

There was an uncomfortable silence.

'I expect you wonder why I'm here?' he demanded at length. 'You must be getting quite sick of me bursting in on your privacy. You had already refused to have dinner with me. I shall understand if you're extremely angry with me. You might even interpret my unannounced visit as spying.'

'Nothing of the kind,' she said weakly. 'I'm sure you always have good reason for calling on me. I wanted an early night because I felt rotten, and that's the truth. The only caller I expected was Dr Bute, but you're very welcome.'

'You—er—mean Crawley wasn't expected?'

'Of course he wasn't. I left the door on the latch for the doctor and Tony sneaked in.'

'If Dr Crawley's attentions are ever unwelcome you must let me know and I'll—'

Celia's lips quirked into a smile. 'Would you really knock his teeth in? How delightful!'

'I have a good left hook,' he informed her, 'but one scarcely ever needs resort to violence.'

'Don't worry,' she told him. 'I can handle Tony. When I'm fighting fit, that is.'

'And when you're not?' he asked softly.

'You wanted to see me,' she brushed this off. 'I have a throat like gravel. Shall I make some coffee?'

'Have hot lemon. I'll join you. I think I'm getting this thing too.'

As they sipped she said, 'Before you discuss your business, I have something to show you. You asked me to keep you

124

informed.'

She gave him the letter which had arrived that morning.

'It looks bad, doesn't it?' she asked him. 'They make it sound so horrible having a child living in London. I can't deny we have smogs or that it's grimy. I feel depressed about it, as though I've lost the darling already.'

'You would mind that terribly, Celia?'

'Yes, I would. There are minor pinpricks about bringing up a child, of course. I'm tied. When I think of holidays I'll have to go somewhere I know she'll be happy, such as the seaside. I can't have a lie-in at weekends, she's such an early bird and there's no peace once she's awake. Even so, I should be torn in half if they took her away from me. But what can I do?'

'You could live in the country. We have perfectly good clean country an hour out of London. Lots of people commute quite successfully every day.'

'The green belt, you mean? I couldn't possibly afford to buy a house there. They don't call it the stockbroker belt for nothing.'

'I could afford a house.'

'But—but—' she tried to read his countenance and failed. 'What are you suggesting, Dr Grainger?' she asked formally. 'I don't understand you.'

'Nothing sordid,' he assured her. 'I've

thought for some time of offering you and Fiona a home. I want you to be my wife, Celia.'

'Oh,' she said weakly, and felt so peculiar she was sure her temperature had soared to a hundred and two in an instant. 'Oh, dear. I don't know what to say.'

'Well, of course you're surprised, but I sincerely hope not shocked? I hope I may be allowed to state my case, or would you rather we deferred our talk? You're not very well—'

'No, please do go on,' Celia urged. A thousand echoes were still coming back to her from all corners of the room, 'I want you to be my wife—my wife—wife—wife.' She had never heard such a sweet phrase in all her life before. Naturally she wanted to hear the theme developed into a declaration of love. That would make her day—and her life.

'I've now known you six months, Celia, and you're—well, a very attractive and nice person. I like being with you. I've even wanted to say things I had no right to, because you made it clear that, to you, falling in love with a person was the open sesame to such overtures. I knew, with regret, that we had not fallen in love in that way. To me, our special friendship was much more precious and enduring. To like a person, to want to be with that person at all times, that is a much sounder basis for marriage, which is an enduring thing rather that a heightening of awareness at a certain time of moon. Today I felt I had to make all this quite clear to you. Whatever I do feel for you, and it's strong and persistent in me, does not allow for other men to enter your bedroom and force their attentions upon you. I resent that very much and you will either grant, or deny, me the right to feel so about you when you give me your answer. You must think about it, of course, but I hope you won't be too long coming to a decision. Shall I go now?'

'No, please stay a little while longer.'

'He little knows I have nothing to hesitate about,' thought Celia. 'I'm in love with him, no matter what he feels about me, and it would be looking a gift-horse in the mouth to refuse him.'

'Would it be a real marriage, and I think you know what I mean by that?' she asked him frankly.

'I'm sure we would both want it to be—in time,' he gently assured her, and for the first time in their acquaintance he deliberately made a physical contact by taking her hand and squeezing it in his own. He couldn't have known how more needles of awareness shot through her in that moment than from all Tony's ravishing caresses. 'The act of love, for want of a better description, comes very naturally to most people. I would never force anything on you,' he assured her.

'But just supposing I disappoint you in that

127

respect,' she insisted, 'and let's face it, most couples know their physical reactions before they go to the altar. What would you get out of it?'

'Celia,' he said in exasperation, 'you've not just a beautiful body, you know. You have a quicksilver mind, a delightful humour and I find you stimulating company. You can't have much opinion of my manhood if you imagine I should fail to be interested in you, having made up my mind to it. I shall be well content with anything you can give. Also I can share Fiona, if we're allowed to keep her.'

With a little pang of disappointment she realised that he was expecting Fiona along with her.

'Supposing we can't,' she murmured, 'and you're stuck with me?'

'Then we could console one another. Maybe it wouldn't be the end of the world, or of us, or of a family. But let us believe we would be allowed to keep Fiona, arguing our case from strength and a house in the country.'

'And my work?' she whispered.

'Oh, that must go on as long as you wish. We won't let anybody push a promising young medico—or should that be medica?—from her true vocation. You needn't work so hard or long, though. The grocer will still be paid. Now I would like to say, Celia, that no matter what you decide

128

I'm happy that you didn't say no immediately, or show any revulsion towards me. But if you do decide against me your job will still be quite secure and you can count on my friendship. Goodnight. Don't come in tomorrow unless you're fit.'

'I'll be in,' she said confidently. 'Goodnight, Alan.'

'Don't get cold,' he said at the door, and still hesitated, looking down at her.

On impulse she reached up and kissed him. His lips were a shock. They were firm and yet gentle, and she found herself urging them to accept her tribute, not to misunderstand, and after a moment warmth from him crept through her veins like a transfusion.

'I—I thought we ought to make a—a—start,' she explained as she sank down from her tip-toes feeling very small and feminine.

'Yes, a good idea.' He patted her cheek and was gone, leaving her to lean against the closed door in agonies of heaven and hell and all stages between. Was it enough for one to love and another merely to like and enjoy?

'I was completely lost the minute he said he wanted me for his wife,' she thought feverishly. 'If he doesn't go all the way to falling in love with me I shall probably die, but I've got to say yes and chance everything. It's got to be yes. Oh, dear! I think I might die tonight, the way I feel, and perhaps that might not be a bad thing. At least he'll be sorry, as things are now, and I can go to heaven happy without any thought of having wronged him or myself.'

*　　　*　　　*

The spring sun was shining into the south-facing windows of Harley Street, kissing the daffodils and hyacinths cheerfully glowing from window-boxes and decorative displays and creating an illusion of open spaces and country freshness.

Celia, feeling unreasonably happy, knocked on the door of her senior's consulting room and entered. Here shone the sun; her own room was dim in comparison; and she shone back at it, smiling and hoping it would still be like this tomorrow.

'Well, that's it, sir,' she reported, placing two file covers on the desk and putting her hands in the pockets of her loose white coat in a relaxed way. 'I hope there's nothing I've left undone.'

Dr Wilkes-Mather smiled in an understanding way. Celia liked her new boss very much. He was middle-aged and knowledgeable and moved through his days unhurried and competent. He was married, with a family of sons, all following in father's footsteps. One of these, Guy, was stepping in to act as locum in Celia's absence on honeymoon, though both father and son agreed that it was a much better idea to work apart from the family as a general rule.

'I'm sure you're to be excused if you have, my dear,' her principal smiled. 'It's the big day tomorrow, isn't it? You're having this afternoon off.'

'I still have to have a final fitting for the suit I'm wearing,' Celia said breathlessly, 'and there are a thousand things to be done. I don't know whether I'm on my head or my heels.'

'Weddings are inclined to do that to one,' Dr Wilkes-Mather told her. 'Is all settled at your new home?'

'Oh, yes. Fortunately the house was in very good condition and only the nursery needed repapering. The gardener stayed on and we have a very good house-keeper. Also I came to a marvellous arrangement with Mrs Fern, who has been looking after Fiona for me. She is a widow with a small boy, you know, and finds it hard going sometimes to make ends meet. There's a flat over the garage at the house, however, which the previous owners provided for their chauffeur. We won't need a chauffeur, and Mrs Fern was delighted to move out of London and occupy the flat. She thinks it will be better for Billy and the two children will still have one another. Everything has really worked out splendidly, and the train service is so good I don't find living in the Chalfont area at all inconvenient. Alan has managed everything marvellously.' She sighed with happiness.

'I suppose he'll be quite eager to move into the house, too,' the man said significantly.

'Yes,' Celia flushed slightly. 'He intends keeping on the London flat for the time being as it will be useful having a pied-à-terre when he is on special research and can't get home at a reasonable time. Well, I could talk about it all day, but I suppose I'd better go. Thank you for letting me off, sir.'

'You've worked in this practice for more than a year, my dear, and have a right to leave. I'll see you in a month, then? Oh, my wife thought you might like to have this. We've never dared use it, but I hope you will have the courage to do so. There's nothing more frustrating to beautiful things than collecting dust in cupboards, I'm sure.'

Celia gasped over the exquisite Spode coffee-service set out in its velvet-lined box before her.

'Oh, sir!'

'And much happiness to go with it.' The large, firm hand mangled hers for an instant. 'I'm sure that goes without saying, knowing you and Alan.'

Celia felt a little tearful on the way home to Little Chalfont where she detrained, took her car from the park and motored downhill to beautiful Chalfont St Giles and Mildhaven, the impressive house set in two glorious acres, mostly woodland, which was such a paradise for children to grow up in. She had only been living in the house, herself, for two weeks and she still marvelled as she saw the sweeping circular drive, the golden wash of daffodils, the virgin heads of narcissi and a pink, so far nameless creeper dripping over the mellowed brick of the house itself. It was not as big as it looked, the house. It had impressive width but was not very deep. The housekeeper had a bed-sitting room and her own bathroom behind the kitchen, looking on to the back garden. There were two reception rooms and a study on the ground floor and four bedrooms and bathroom upstairs. One of the rooms had been converted for Fiona's use, though while her aunt was away she would be sharing Billy's bedroom, to which she was looking forward enormously.

'We both going on holiday,' she liked to say. 'I'm staying with Billy and Fernie and you're staying with Uncle Alan.'

Celia's limbs turned to water when she thought of the significance of 'staying with Uncle Alan,' but she supposed all brides must feel the same, nervous and excited and driven by a sense of absolute inevitability towards the final physical capitulation.

So much had happened since Alan's proposal and her acceptance that she hadn't really had time to think much of the personal

133

relationship between them. Alan was gratified by her acceptance, she knew, and in a controlled way he seemed excited, too. But he demonstrated his excitement through things rather than feelings. He had found just the house, he told her, and one Thursday afternoon they drove out to see it and she was captivated and the deal was finalised with extreme urgency to suit their needs. Then Alan excitedly transferred his bride-to-be to the house, along with her charge and devoted little retinue. Everybody was happy, and still the magic words 'I love you' did not pass Alan's lips.

'If only he would say it everything would be perfect,' Celia pondered.

There was a serious little consultation about the wedding. Did she want a church ceremony or should they be married in Caxton Hall?

'I'll leave all that to you, Alan,' Celia told him.

She was vaguely disappointed when it was to be the registrar who was to join them in wedlock.

Another conversation elicited the fact that there was nobody she wished to invite to the ceremony.

'All my friends are far too scattered and we only correspond at Christmas. I have no close relatives, only second cousins and one great-aunt. I think after the wedding will be time enough to tell them.'

'Oh. Then I'll just rope in a couple of my colleagues as witnesses. Perhaps, as it's going to be such a quiet wedding, you would come with me next Sunday to see my mother?'

Celia felt startled at this. She hadn't thought that Alan might have relatives who would be interested in his marriage. She vaguely remembered that he had mentioned his mother on the day of Reggie's funeral.

'Supposing she disapproves of me at this eleventh hour?' she asked lightly.

'If she does she won't let it make any difference. We'll still be given a very nice tea with plenty of home-mades. Her companion, of many years' standing, has an implicit belief in the practice of serving calories to cement human relationships. Both dear ladies, are, needless to say, as thin as rakes.'

So Celia had met Mrs Grainger and liked her on sight. She was Reggie's mother, too, and they had spoken of him.

'He was a dear boy,' the elderly woman stated firmly, and patted Alan on the shoulder. 'I was blessed with two dear boys,' she said fondly.

Alan winked at Celia.

'So now you know I can always run home to Mother,' he said through a froth of éclair, and they all laughed delightedly.

Coming home on this spring afternoon, the day before her wedding, Celia felt that everything would be so perfect if only Alan was as deeply in love with her as she was with him. It was a rub that he was marrying her hopefully rather than having arrived. He was fond of her, and nowadays when they kissed there was nothing remotely brotherly about the salute, but she still tormented herself with the idea that there was a second-best flavour about their relationship.

'After tomorrow it will be better,' she told herself, putting her own door key into her own front door and surveying the splendour of the oak-panelled hall and the shining golden parquet of the floor.

'Dr Derwent? You're home.' Mrs Borridge, the housekeeper, was at hand to relieve her of her parcels, including the priceless coffee-set.

'Set it out with the other things,' Celia bade the woman, 'and keep the children out of that room.'

'Certainly, Doctor. I'll bring your lunch into the dining room, now. I take it Dr Grainger isn't coming along today?'

'No. He has too much winding up to do. Far more than I have, and I shall be busy enough.'

It was luxury having someone waiting on one after the mad scrambles of getting home to Fiona and setting to making meals and running baths and washing clothes. She still saw a lot of the child, but they were relaxed hours they spent together and purely enjoyable.

After a leisurely lunch she was fitted for her wedding suit, and it was perfect. It was a powder blue fine wool and suited her to perfection. She was wondering whether it was the right thing for a register office when Mrs Borridge tapped on the bedroom door.

'Doctor, there's a Dr Raven called to see you. Are you expecting her?'

CHAPTER TEN

Her attention divided between the suit and the house-keeper, Celia murmured, 'Raven? Raven? I seem to think that rings a bell somewhere.' The bell rang finally and she felt herself blanch with a feeling of shock. 'Dr Raven here to see me? Please show her into the sitting room, Mrs Borridge. I'll be down in a moment.'

She reminded herself that Denise Raven was Alan's ex-wife. She got no pleasure out of the knowledge, but it was an acknowledged fact and a disturbing one. Dr Raven's presence here today could only mean that she knew about the wedding. But in what kind of mood had she come? The only way of finding out was to face her, but it was a nerve-racking moment opening the door into the sitting room and trying to appear welcoming and utterly composed.

'How do you do, Dr Raven. This is a surprise.'

'I'm sure it is, my dear, but I had to come and offer my congratulations. I never thought that day we had our little chat that you were Alan's intended bride.'

'Didn't you?' Celia laughed as lightly as she could. 'At that time I'm not sure I was. Can I offer you anything? Tea?'

'Sherry would be most acceptable. I haven't had a drink today.'

Denise Raven was really superb, Celia decided, as she rose to pour sherry from the side-table in the window embrasure. She was the type of woman who looked her best in suits, and knew it. Today's was a pale lilac silk jersey with black accessories including a carelessly draped sable stole. Her face was discreetly and beautifully made up. Everything about her was controlled and poised apart from the restless, darting black eyes.

'You must be curious as to the reason for my visit,' said Dr Raven. 'I know I would be in your place.'

'Yes, I suppose I am. How did you know about us—Alan and me?'

'They do publish intention of marriage, my dear! It wasn't difficult. I'm also quite an experienced detective when I want to be. I

138

don't think Alan need be told about this visit, do you? I'm sure he would misunderstand my motives.'

'Oh? Well, that makes it rather awkward. I don't want to start by having secrets from him.'

'How sweetly naive! If we women didn't have some secrets life would be absolutely intolerable. I know my visit to be perfectly innocent in intent. After all, I've been married to Alan and I think I can give you a few hints on how to make him happy. If you can avoid the pitfalls which broke us up then I'll be happy for you.'

Celia found herself waiting, listening for more, as though an oracle were speaking.

'Give him a child as soon as possible,' Denise Raven advised, lighting a cigarette and fixing it in a long, jade holder.

Celia flushed.

'I don't know about that,' she said in some embarrassment. 'I have my career to think of.'

'If you value your marriage forget your career until you've done your wifely duty. With a baby in the nursery you can go ahead and do what you like. Alan is a frustrated parent, and in my job I should know what I'm talking about.'

Celia resented having a third party filling the nursery for her, and spoke up.

'I know Alan is fond of children. He's

devoted to my small niece.'

'You'll find that won't be sufficient. I suggested adopting a child and he went up in the air. My career, too, was important, and I sacrificed my marriage for it. I'm a very strong-minded woman and happen to believe in myself and my work. Give him a child. Think of yourself as the Grainger stud farm, in the nicest possible way, and all will be well.'

The black eyes were lowered before their gleam of triumph could be revealed. Celia was shocked.

'I don't think we ought to discuss such matters together, Dr Raven. If you made mistakes when you were married to Alan I expect I will, too, but they're not your business. I don't want to anticipate crises. Tomorrow is my wedding day, and—'

'You're in love with him, aren't you?' the other woman asked.

Celia's revealing blush was answer enough.

'Good! He'll like that. Men enjoy being adored. It's very true what they say, you know, about man's love being of man's life a thing apart. They can turn it on and off like their charm, at will. I'm sure you'll be sensible. You look a sensible girl. I know you must be busy and I don't intend taking up your time any longer. Goodbye, Dr Derwent. I'm glad I can still call you that. I'm a great believer in personal identities. So many women lose theirs when they marry.'

Celia watched the sleek black Jensen creep out of the drive like a horrible slug, leaving something nasty behind it. Until Dr Raven had actually left, the room purged of her presence, she couldn't make up her mind whether the visit had been made in innocence or with a dangerous and damaging intent.

Damaging the visit certainly had been, whether it was intended or not. Whereas Celia had been content to go ahead with an arrangement which allowed her to pour out her own frustrated affections into the receptacle for which they had been created and intended, seeking to win love back if it was true that loving begat love, yet she was totally unprepared to perpetuate a union it had been decided was barely in flower, let alone ready for fruition.

They were hastening to the wedding nominally for convenience' sake. Next month the court would hear the claimants for Fiona's guardianship. Alan Grainger had assured her that, married to him, and in this new setting he had provided, she had a very good case indeed for being allowed to keep Fiona. Now a horrid little doubt crept in that Fiona might well be the excuse which gave Alan legal rights to make physical demands upon her before she was mentally prepared for this. He had told her that 'all that sort of thing' would be to the tune of her calling, but he had also

141

said that he would be a poor sort of man if he could not persuade her interest in a physical relationship. He spoke of it as though it was not the all-important part of marriage, but after they were married might he not decide it was a part well worth the investigating?

She felt rather foolish as she remembered that he had allowed her to make the running in physical salutations so far. She had thought him shy and had actually said, 'I thought we ought to make a start' when she had first laid her lips against his. Since then they had kissed often, but always she had indicated her willingness and made the first move; always he had been restrained and controlled; yet she had gained the impression that behind the control was the power of a vast dam of emotion waiting to be unleashed. These things had excited and intrigued her, now she found herself regarding the unknown quantities of this man with a certain amount of trepidation and grim anticipation.

Denise Raven had sown seeds of doubt she could not have dreamed of. Breathing in the ear of a young woman pleasantly nervous of all the changes in her life that marriage promised, she had virtually cut the ground from under her listener's feet.

'I can still say no,' Celia told herself in panic, 'there's still time.'

But when she looked round she felt trapped. Here she already was established in

Alan's house; here was Fiona happily settled and Mrs Fern and Billy uprooted and planted more salubriously; Mrs Borridge had left a job with a widower because she preferred to work in a 'family' atmosphere. So many people would be inconvenienced by her turning back from the altar that she boggled at the very idea and at last asked herself if she was not, perhaps, being a little foolish.

When Alan telephoned, as he had promised, at a little after eight o'clock, he seemed to sense all was not well.

'Nervous, Celia?'

'Oh, yes. Yes!' She longed to tell him the reason for this state of nerves, but there had been a challenge about Denise Raven when she had suggested Alan need not be told of the visit. 'What would you do if I didn't turn up tomorrow?'

It was a stupid question and she regretted it the very next moment.

'I would much rather you informed me now, if that's your intention,' he told her, and added softly, 'What's the matter? Cold feet?'

'Yes. I suppose it's natural?'

'It is. Mine aren't too warm, either.'

'We'd both better wear bedsocks tonight,' she faltered, and felt a sudden closeness to him, as though they trembled together on the brink of something almost too big and adventurous to contemplate. 'How terrible if it was you who wasn't there!' she decided.

143

'I would never let you down, Celia,' he told her sincerely. 'I'll be there if you want me to be.'

Again she felt a niggle of resentment that he had put the ball once again in her court. They would kiss only when she was ready to; they would marry only if she really wished it.

'I suppose it is a bit late to turn back—' she said almost to herself.

'Look, Celia,' he was standing no more nonsense and she knew it, 'do you want me to come over? Is there anything else to discuss? I'm not exactly kidnapping you, you know.'

'No,' she pulled herself together sharply. 'You must have plenty to do, and I'm being stupid. I shall have an early night and take a sleeping pill.'

'Goodnight—till it be morrow.'

She hadn't suspected this streak of romanticism in him and felt pleasantly surprised. Research Fellows were more readily associated with hard facts than poetic phrases.

Celia undressed feeling much more settled. Denise was no friend of hers and she would no longer fear her. Whatever had happened to wreck that marriage must not be allowed to be contagious. There would be no quarrel over children. When the time was ripe she would be proud and happy to start a family. Wasn't she already in love with Alan and longing for him to feel the same way about her? Talk of stud farms and suchlike was ugly and damaging in the context of human relationships.

She took her pill and allowed her mind to drift in sedative channels until she was on the brink of sleep, and then a stark thought struck her brain like a gong rousing her to sudden wakefulness. One such night Denise Raven must have lain thinking of Alan and her wedding on the morrow. It could never be a unique experience marrying Dr Grainger as it had all happened before.

After this Celia lay wakeful for most of the long night. It was dawn before she slipped into an uneasy doze, and at seven-thirty Fiona crept into bed beside her, entwined her slim little arms about her and said confidingly, 'This is the day we both going on our holidays, isn't it, Aunty Celia?'

'That's right, darling.'

It was April the eleventh and there was no sun. The heavens lowered with an April threat of rain and the daffodils hung heavy from the night's showers.

'I wish I was coming with you, Aunty C.'

In reply Celia hugged the child to her fiercely.

'So do I, poppet. I shall look forward to coming back to you.'

Somehow in her heart she felt sure that she had spoken truly. She would be so glad to get back to what she knew from some nameless dread she feared.

★   ★   ★

The marriage ceremony, civil style, was nonetheless impressive. Celia looked pale and pretty in her new suit and went through all the motions like a figure in a dream. Alan looked very smart in a Savile Row suit, and his good looks, when he was groomed as now, almost hurt the eyes. Celia was introduced to two names revered in the world of medicine, which were attached to the official document as witnesses, and these two persons insisted on doing the honours of drinking a toast to the newly-weds at a nearby exclusive bar.

Throughout all this Celia nodded and smiled like a puppet. She felt very tired and subdued, unable to raise the smallest feeling of excitement for either the occasion, its celebration or, when they reached London Airport, the great silver aeroplane standing out on the tarmac waiting to wing them out into the wide blue yonder.

She was occasionally aware of Alan's hand on her arm, helping her into a hired car and to alight, and once she heard his voice announce, 'Dr and Mrs Grainger.' It may have been her imagination at work putting that slight emphasis on the Mrs, and she realised with a sense of shock that it referred to her and that she was his to do with as he

146

willed.

'May I know where we're going?' she forced herself to ask banteringly as they waited in the reception hall at the airport.

'I'm sorry I had to keep you in the dark, Celia,' he told her honestly. 'At such short notice I had to leave things in the hands of the travel agents. All I specified was sun and peace. They assure me that both are to be found in Southern Spain at a place called Torre Nueva. I've taken a furnished villa there.'

'What do we want peace for?' she asked in a hard, bright voice. 'Anybody would think getting married was a battle from which one needed to recuperate.'

He gave her an odd, assessing glance.

'I'm sure we can find whatever you want, Celia. Let's get there and see.'

She felt reproved and knew that she had deserved it. He, too, must be wondering what to expect now that he had taken her on. You couldn't be sure, having made one hash, that you weren't about to make another one.

Walking out to the plane she tried talking about Mr Percival Richard, the famous neuro-surgeon, who had been one of the witnesses of the marriage. Sir Harry Cotoneaster, a bacteriologist, had been the other.

'Mr Richard once gave me a viva,' she told him, 'and I couldn't answer a thing correctly.

How he passed me I'll never know. The men students swore that he had an eye for a pretty ankle and I had to thank that for my success. I never thought I'd find myself hobnobbing with him on terms of equality. Is he still at Bennett's?'

'No. He only lectures now.'

'Sir Harry's a darling little man. He once nearly killed himself doing an experiment, didn't he? I read it in an *M.J.*'

They were bowed aboard the plane, shown to their seats. As Celia leaned back she felt Alan's arm and shot forward as though it had burned her.

'I'm so sorry.' He removed the arm and gave her a wry little smile half of apology and half amusement.

The plane taxied forward and then seemed to become airborne in a great rush. Celia closed her eyes and swallowed as her head buzzed. When she opened them again the cabin was filled with sunlight and the plane was still climbing from a grey, woolly carpet which covered the ground beneath them.

'My!' she gave a little gasp. 'It's years since I flew. I thought I was being left behind for a moment there.'

'Are you aware that you're being shone on, Celia, at long last?' he said.

'Not only me, surely? The sun's shining on everybody down this side.'

'I'm sure they're not all brides.' She looked

148

at him quickly. 'I'm sorry. Forget it,' he told her.

She was nervous, and this great silver monster with the speed of an arrow was taking them nearer and nearer to that villa in Torre Nueva, wherever that was, with its peace and seclusion in the sun and all that went with such a situation.

'Just supposing,' she said, when she fancied they had been silent overlong, 'that we lose our claim to Fiona in spite of all. What will we do?'

'What is there to do?' he asked her. 'The law is the law. But why anticipate?'

'I meant could we apply to a higher court, sort of appeal . . . ?'

'I'll find out when and if it happens.'

He said this so peremptorily that she stiffened.

'Oh, well, if you don't want to talk why don't you say so?'

'Celia, on my wedding day I don't want to talk about either Percy Richard's past idiosyncrasies or unpleasant legal possibilities. I want to talk about us.'

'Very well, Alan. What about us?'

'We both did turn up this morning, so we've started something, haven't we?'

'I suppose we have,' her voice wobbled.

'It hasn't been an absolutely wonderful day up to now, has it?'

'No. Are they usually wonderful? I mean

149

you should know, you've been married before.'

'Is that suddenly needling you?'

'No, not that.'

'Then what is? You've obviously got something on your chest.'

'Alan, I'm tired. After a night's sleep I'll feel much better. I've been in a dream all day.'

He took her hand and held it firmly.

'Close your eyes and relax now,' he urged.

'Very well, I will.'

That handclasp was comforting and committing, she pondered as she reclined back in her seat. It was really his hand now; the hand she had given him in marriage. They hadn't kissed since the ceremony, she realised; there hadn't been much opportunity for one thing and, if he was still leaving the initiative to her, she hadn't been forthcoming.

If only that black-eyed woman hadn't called like a witch to cast a spell of doubt over everything today would have been very much happier. Her own dark thoughts had somehow communicated to Alan, her husband, and he was as uncertain of the future as was she. When they reached the villa, when they were alone, they must talk, discover what their relationship was to be. Yesterday, when she had left Harley Street, she had known; now, today, she was utterly confused and uncertain.

She was surprised to learn that she had actually slept. Alan was shaking her gently, saying, 'Fasten your seat-belt, dear. We're over Malaga airport now.'

CHAPTER ELEVEN

A hired car was handed over to the newly-weds once the formalities of customs and immigration were over. Everything had been very well organised by the travel agents, even down to a marked map giving directions on how to reach Torre Nueva. This was a small village nestling in a fold of the lower Sierras, grapevine country, with a river tumbling through a ravine towards the silver line of the sea which shone on the distant horizon about three miles away. The villa was European-owned but built and furnished in Andalusian style and it looked very white and appealing in the early evening light. A maid was on hand to show them round and give them their evening meal. She spoke English haltingly and attractively.

'Please to tell I make comic mistakes,' she implored, 'so my English is more good.'

'Silly mistakes, Carmela,' Celia promptly obliged, 'and your English will be better, not more good.'

'T'ank you, señora. I will write in my little

book.'

'It's a lovely villa and a glorious setting, Alan,' Celia felt bound to say. There was an enormous bed in a room overlooking the ravine upon which Carmela had laid out a diaphanous blue nightdress and a pair of mauve pyjamas. She didn't want to think of the intimacy of those garments lying there together. It was all too soon and she wasn't ready. She would refuse to be rushed.

After a very nice dinner which they both enjoyed, it being the first real meal of that long day, Carmela washed up and went off home. Normally, she told them, she finished at half-past six. Another day she would prepare the meal and cook it, if they wanted to dine at the house, and leave them to serve for themselves. The washing-up could always wait until morning.

'I think that's a hint that we ought to dine out,' Alan smiled after she had gone. 'We'll have a look round tomorrow and make some plans. How do you fancy Flamenco with your paella?'

'It sounds delightful,' Celia agreed.

'Come and sit over here,' he urged, patting the settee beside him, 'wife,' he added meaningly.

She walked over to him dutifully and did not protest when his arms drew her close and he kissed her.

'Hm!' he murmured a few minutes later. 'It

has been a long day. I shall have a bath and go to bed. How about you?'

'I'll smoke a cigarette, I think, and then go to bed, too,'

She smoked one cigarette, two, and helped herself to a glass of sherry from the bottle on the sideboard. After this she decided she had better get what now promised to be an ordeal over, and went into the big bedroom. The mauve pyjamas had disappeared, though, of course, Alan had probably taken them into the bathroom with him. She could hear him still splashing and humming softly.

She undressed quickly and donned the nightdress and a negligée, afterwards folding up her clothes and putting them away neatly. Alan was a very long time. She climbed into bed and lay gazing back at a sickle moon which stared inquisitively at her through the window.

She jumped in amazement as a tap came on the door.

'I wondered if you were still awake, Celia. I wanted to say goodnight.'

'Goodnight,' she called back before she realised that her husband did not intend coming to her at all. Her fears and dreads of physical trespass, which had haunted and ruined the whole day, thanks to Denise Raven's oblique statements and cruel innuendoes, were totally unfounded. Alan had no intention of forcing any situation upon her to which she was not a co-operative and willing partner.

After a few moments of thought, all idea of sleep having deserted her, she began arbitrarily to resent the situation. Was it right that a newly-married woman should sleep alone on her wedding night? Was there something wrong with her? Was sex-appeal missing from her make-up?

She knew she was quite normal in this respect. Tony found her very desirable. But whereas Tony was inclined to behave with the blind instinct of a young buck, Alan Grainger apparently had no instincts but those of a gentleman. Was he leaving all to her, as he had the kissing and the marrying? Was he at this moment lying awake and wondering at the many creaks of the big, comfortable bed, or was he fast asleep, his thoughts unsullied by perfectly natural desires?

'Please let him come to me!' Celia begged the moon as she made to hide behind a peak of the High Sierra. But Alan didn't come and at two o'clock in the morning Celia went in search of him. She found him stretched out on a chaise-longue in the guest-room, the bed of which had not, for obvious reasons, been made up. She knew he was not asleep, for a freshly stubbed out cigarette still glowed and smoked in the darkness.

'Alan!' her note of appeal brought him to his feet. 'I can't sleep,' she added lamely.

He found her without switching on the light, for which she was grateful.

'I hope I didn't disturb you,' he said softly. 'I've been reading. I couldn't sleep either.'

'I should think not on that thing, and it's cold in here. At least you should have looked out some sheets and blankets. There must be thousands packed away somewhere.'

'I suppose I didn't think of it,' he told her, but she felt a bond of understanding with him and knew, as though he had confided in her, that he had thought about making up the bed and rejected the idea because of Carmela. If the maid had caught him there, in the morning, the peculiar ways of the newly-wed English would soon be the gossip of the village.

'There's a great big bed through there going to waste,' she ventured, and shivered.

His hands felt her and his voice exclaimed in wonder.

'You'll catch cold, Celia. You've hardly anything on. Off you go to bed.'

'You, too. After all, we are married now.'

She thought afterwards, just before sliding into a deep and contented sleep, 'He was right, bless him! He left it all to me. I don't know what Denise was talking about. He's an absolutely wonderful husband, considerate, kind and tremendously exciting. I want to make him happy more than anything in the world.'

155

Though April nights in Southern Spain can be cold with thin winds blowing off the High Sierra, the days are warm as an English July. Roses are in bloom and peasant women trot from villa to villa selling baskets of dew-wet strawberries.

Celia awoke to feel a bar of golden sunlight lying across her face like a warm arm; another warm arm lay across her body, relaxed and pleasantly possessive. Her brain felt clearer than for some days, as though nagging doubts had finally been removed leaving the whole of life as plain as a pikestaff.

It had been a terrible mistake to allow somebody from the past to intrude upon what was the business of two people in the present. She would make it all up to Alan from now on. His wedding day had not been particularly propitious, but that could be accounted to nerves, and henceforward she would see to it that he had no complaint.

She looked at him as for the first time, through eyes dewy with remembered tenderness and passion. Perhaps even now there was the seed of a child in her. She rather hoped so. Her career as a married woman was really more important than her career as a doctor this morning. If Alan wanted a child, what was wrong with that?

When a man desired a child he chose someone special to be its mother. Therefore, if he was not yet terribly in love with her he had at least exalted her by giving her his name and the opportunity of bearing his child.

She slid slowly, gingerly from under that restraining arm and held her breath as he groaned softly, 'Darling!'

His hair was dark and tousled against the snow-white of the pillow and small beads of sweat stood on his brow.

She took a shower and dressed. It was only half-past seven and already she knew this was to be a good day. Mildhaven, Harley Street, even Fiona seemed to have receded into another dimension. This was the small and yet infinite world of Alan and Celia, learning how to love and finding it an absorbing occupation, walking together in the sun that might just as well have been their exclusive and captive luminary, and commanding time to await their tarrying.

Singing in the kitchen, softly and happily, she busied herself making an English type breakfast on the butane-gas cooker.

'Good morning!' Alan's voice came significantly from the doorway, and she blushed because the way he said it recalled last night. She left the bacon spluttering and ran to him, her lips ready, her body soft and pliant against his.

'Missus!' he suddenly laughed into her

hair. 'Something is about to explode over there.'

She ran back to the bacon which was crinkling up into nothingness and turned down the flame so that it went out with a plop.

'Oh, damn! she exclaimed. 'I didn't mean it to do that. Alan, make yourself useful and set the table on the verandah, instead of standing there grinning like a Cheshire cat. Oh, look! The funny little Spanish matches made out of wax. Are they short of wood, then?'

On his way with plates and knives and forks he saluted her on the back of the neck.

'You have tiny curls here,' he said in some wonderment, 'all innocent and little-girlish.'

'Then they're telling lies,' she decided, 'because I'm really quite a big girl, aren't I?'

She looked at him with a mixture of shyness and boldness.

'Yes,' he looked back at her meaningfully, 'you've grown recently. Watch out you don't burn those eggs!'

'Men!' she sighed complacently, as a married woman will, 'always thinking about their tummies.'

He loomed over her darkly all of a sudden.

'When did Carmela say she would be coming?'

'In about five minutes.'

'For that reason only I will allow my

thoughts to be of gluttony, but in future, young woman, watch out!'

* * *

They made love, they walked many miles in companionable harmony, they wined and dined in places with names like El Caballo Blanco and La Parra and made love again; they drove for miles to dream-wonder places called Granada and Ronda and Nerja, and with the onset of night, with the moon growing larger and more inquisitive, they forgot all they had seen in the wonderment of rediscovering one another, which was at once so complete an experience that, temporarily, all else was blotted out.

The second week advanced and for the first time during their stay at the Villa Mañana Alan looked soberly across the breakfast table at his wife, neatly segmenting a grapefruit. They had got over the bacon and egg stage some days ago. It was Carmela's day off. There was a *fiesta* for Palm Sunday and she had invited them to go along and see the procession, which was to be '*muy, muy grande.*'

'Celia,' he said rather uncomfortably, 'have you thought about the possibility of our having a family?'

'Yes,' she smiled happily. 'Staggering, isn't it?'

159

'Be serious, dear,' he gently rebuked her. 'I must confess that happiness such as I've found with you is inclined to make one a little selfish. I certainly hope you won't have a baby on account of it.'

Her eyebrows shot up in surprise.

'But I thought that was the idea,' she returned. 'I want us to have a baby.'

He hushed her lips with a finger as he would a child, with gentle admonishment.

'Celia, you're so very sweet and terribly impractical. I never suspected you could be such a dear little addle-head and tempt me to be one too. You're sitting for your Membership in the late autumn and need to do a lot of studying and attend lectures. It would be impossible to do this with the added inconvenience of a first pregnancy. Also there's Wilkes-Mather to consider, and your job. Our own natural desires must be sublimated for a time. It's been wonderful, darling, but—' his sigh was expressive yet final.

She felt strangely aggrieved and shaken to think that he could put his feet so firmly back on earth again as to think of these things.

'I thought the whole idea was that you desperately wanted a child,' she said, feeling somehow near to tears. 'Denise said—'

If she had thrown a grenade under the table she could not have achieved a more explosive effect than mentioning that name. She immediately realised her blunder, but could not recall it.

'When did you see Denise Raven?' he asked in a voice which petrified.

'She—she came to see me at Mildhaven the day before the wedding,' Celia stammered, knowing that only the truth would satisfy this man who had suddenly turned into a stranger before her eyes. 'She wished me luck—all that sort of thing.'

'Why wasn't I told of this visit?'

'Well, she was sure you would misunderstand her motives. She only wanted me to make you happy, Alan.'

'And how was that to be achieved?' he asked inexorably.

'She said you were a frustrated parent and told me to give you a child immediately.'

He stood up, and for a moment, as she saw his tanned knuckles strained white against the chair he was holding, she thought he must crush it into matchwood before her eyes.

'So all this time,' he threw both arms wide significantly, 'has really been on Denise's account? Good for her! Good for the benevolent Dr Raven!'

Celia jumped up, too, worried by the change in him. She grabbed at his shirt and wept miserably.

'Don't be angry, Alan. Please don't be so angry. What's gone wrong? We were so happy. What has Denise coming to see me

161

got to do with it?'

He flung her off as with a sudden distaste.

'Denise has this effect on people. She has everybody examining their motives even for the most natural of events. You were a nice girl prepared to take a big step with me because we were nice people and could be relied on to behave considerately and kindly to one another and stumble into a satisfactory relationship somehow, some day. Denise steps in and says, in effect, "Alan must have what he wants, he's a selfish brute, and what he wants happens to be a child of his own flesh and blood. So you'd better sacrifice your own body and your ambitions and get on with it." I can see it all now. Shock was your first reaction, then doubt and suspicion. Was I really only marrying you for that? You thought of backing out and felt all had gone too far. You were alternately panic-stricken and reassured. Perhaps you thought, I sincerely hope you did, "Well, he isn't such a dreadful beast up to now. He can't turn into Mr Hyde overnight. I'll go ahead and hope for the best." So you turned up at Caxton Hall, looking absolutely petrified, "went through with it" and spent a miserable few hours until, remembering Denise's exhortations, you took the plunge and surrendered yourself to the brute.'

'Oh, Alan,' she moaned miserably, 'it wasn't really like that at the end. I wanted to make you happy because I—because—I—liked you very much. It's true I kept remembering what Denise said and it did unsettle me. I had thought we would have children some day, but I didn't want to be rushed. Well, I didn't know you very well, did I? But now it's different. I've been so wonderfully happy with you, and giving you a child would be my way of saying thank you. Don't you see?'

He handed her his handkerchief to dry her eyes upon. She had been feeling unsuccessfully about her person for her own.

'I want you to be frank with me, Celia,' he said, as doctor to patient. 'Do you think you could be pregnant?'

'I know I'm not,' she said into the handkerchief, with some bitterness, 'if that makes you any happier.'

He sighed in absolute relief and smote his forehead as though to drive black thoughts away.

'Well, thank goodness for that! There's no piper to pay, and we did call quite a merry tune while it lasted.'

She stared at him uncomprehendingly.

'You mean you don't want me any more?'

His grim expression relaxed a little and he lifted her chin with a finger.

'I may want you a lot, but I'm not an animal and I refuse to use you as one. You hit the nail on the head when you said we don't

163

know each other very well, not as one presumes most people who marry do. Well, I would like to know you a lot better, Celia, because all along the line what you offered was nice and wholesome and desirable. I don't want anything inspired by Denise. Understand? In our own time we would have come together as inevitably as river to sea. You need not have trembled for one instant in fear of me. It upsets me to think that you did.' He kissed her gently and caressed her cheeks where they were tear-stained.

'But you were happy with me, Alan? You were really happy, weren't you?'

'Only that you were happy too, Celia. One can't make other people happy. It has to be a joint effort and a shared delight. Yes, I was very happy,' he assured her as her eyes still appealed. 'But I can wait and be patient if you can. We have to think of possible consequences no matter how tempted we may be, having sampled the banquet. Our marriage was arranged to facilitate certain procedures. It didn't have to be rushed from the starting-gate to catch up with others at the risk of life and limb. We'll have our "coronation" when your true maternal instincts catch up with your creditable desire to please me, my dear sweet wife, and you had better keep those undeveloped until you take your Membership. You see, I'm going to dog you into getting that because I'm proud to be married to your bright, probing mind as well as your beautiful, seductive little body.'

She felt happier for this and managed a watery smile.

'I'd forgotten all about work,' she admitted.

'Mañana will do for that,' he told her lightly. 'Now we're going to have a long-overdue talk. I'm going to tell you about Denise, just in case she decides to pay you another visit when I'm not around.'

CHAPTER TWELVE

'I was very much in love with Denise,' Alan began as they stretched out in twin reclining chairs overlooking the ravine through which the swollen river tumbled with muted thunder—obviously it had rained in the hills overnight—'which always makes me suspicious of anyone relying on the permanency of that state nowadays. I was young, barely twenty-five and newly qualified, and she was admittedly thirty. I've never seen her birth certificate; she may be older, but her facial beauty is perennial and I'm sure she'll still be a handsome octogenarian when the time comes. In my eyes she was mature, sophisticated, amusing. I was flattered when she even noticed me and

165

when she actually returned my interest I was completely bowled over. What she saw in me I don't know, but, to judge from my female contemporaries, I had my points as an acceptable escort.

'When I was completely under her spell I asked her to be my wife. I was madly convinced that I could never feel so about anybody else and that she would slip away leaving me desolate unless I did something about it. She took time to think and then gave me her answer. She consented to marry me. I hadn't a well-paid job; I was Surgical Registrar at Highfields at the time, and Denise was attached to the psycho consultant. Denise said we would be all right because she came into a little money when she married. The "little money" turned out to be a sizeable fortune of thirty thousand pounds, but that particular shock came later.

'When I announced my intentions to my family,' he went on, 'there was a fearful row between Reggie and me. He had never been an elder brother in the sense of advising or encouraging me, but he never missed an opportunity of either goading me to anger or belittling my achievements. He was quick to state on this occasion that my adored Denise obviously was benefiting from the marriage in some oblique way or she would never consider attaching herself to such a nonentity. I wouldn't hear such things and I was ready

166

to be offended, and for the first time in our lives we almost came to blows. Mother was upset, as mothers are, by Denise's maturity, but she didn't add to my troubles by raising any objections, bless her!

'The day of the wedding came and I was in a seventh heaven. I took my beautiful bride over to Paris, which was the best I could afford, and there I suffered a shock. Denise, who must long have suspected her feelings, or lack of them, told me she had no interest in the physical side of marriage. She had tried to fall in love previously and could summon up no enthusiasm for the opposite sex or their "boring demands." She was sure I would understand, have patience with her, and if I must have a carnal relationship that I would take care not to involve her in pregnancy. She had to think of her career, she said, and motherhood had never been one of her ambitions. My first reaction was to consider what I had done to her by marrying her, feeling as she did about men. I was sure she was making some kind of horrible sacrifice because she loved me in a pure and spiritual way I did not yet understand. Later I was to wonder what all this would do to me. I was in love, my natural emotions and desires were doomed to frustration and I almost hated myself for having them. I did not, as you may have gathered, attempt to consummate the marriage on her terms, and I was extremely unhappy and confused.'

Celia squeezed his hand chummily here and he gripped back, making her wince.

'You'll never know, my dearest girl, how relieved I was to find your reactions entirely normal that first night. To reject your sweet, tremulous overtures would have been like looking a gift-horse in the mouth, and I daren't remember the joy of knowing you without feeling a little dazed by it all. But to continue with that less happy saga. We came back from Paris and I was installed like a cuckoo in Denise's flat. I still didn't know my function in this peculiar union. I couldn't call myself the breadwinner or—or anything. She earned twice my salary. Then she suddenly came into her "fortune" and my suspicions were aroused. She bought a fabulous new car, refurnished the flat and set about looking for a country cottage. I was feeling a little peeved about this display of wealth; it was becoming so that I could give her nothing which impressed her. My flowers were drowned by displays the florist delivered every week and I was beginning to feel like a "kept" man without any real function in that household.

'Also I was falling rapidly out of love and seeing my "wife" as she really was, a frigid, ambitious, selfish woman, like inferior chocolate in a beautiful box. I had fallen in love with the box and presumed the quality of the goods was equal to the covering. That is why I'm so suspicious of the term, "being in love." It may work out in eighty per cent of relations, but to me it's a temporary state of blindness and insanity.'

Alan decided to light a cigarette and continued.

'Is this boring you? Good! I think you should know the rest. I decided to ask Denise exactly how much she had inherited on her marriage and she told me when I insisted on knowing. "And all thanks to you, darling," she told me with a friendly little pat on the shoulder. "You must ask me if you want any money for odds and ends." This was adding insult to injury and I spoke without thinking through my gall. "Would the platonic state of our relationship have any effect on your inheritance if it were known? Are you really a married woman, Denise? Because I'm thinking of seeking an annulment and leaving you."

'I hadn't really thought of anything of the kind until that moment, but all at once I knew I had to get out of that humiliating situation or learn to hate both her and myself. She played hurt, then angry, then she pleaded. "If you want a child so much, Alan, why don't we adopt one? We can afford it. I'll hire a nanny." I was livid at the very idea. I won't dwell on the sordid details of the arguments and rows which followed. Denise consulted her lawyers and, fortunately for her, the money which had been handed over to her was safely hers on production of the marriage certificate. There was no investigation or strings attached to the future. I was glad about this because I really believed she married me with an eye to this main chance, thinking I was young and malleable and could possibly be kept in a state of suspended adoration indefinitely and only humoured as and when it became unavoidable.

'She didn't want to lose me. In her own way she was fond of me and I was an asset to her. She liked being known as a married woman socially, but she resisted being called Dr Grainger in her hospital and went on working under the name Raven. As the status quo was impossible for me to maintain with any dignity I insisted we must separate. We did so, although Denise urged that we must remain friends, and a little later the marriage was annulled. She has kept tabs on me ever since, friendly ones, I believe. She feels that I was once her possession, like a pet dog which escaped, and of course she's comfortably off, thanks to our experiment, and I suppose feels grateful to me.'

He looked at Celia musingly. 'So why did she seek you out, eh? Ah, here we have the purely female mind at work. I don't think Denise could bring herself to hand me over to a woman who might supply that very need she was unable to meet without some sort of struggle. She took one look at you and knew you could do this—she's very astute—and then she handed you the meat on a platter in such a way as to make your gorge rise against it. She almost succeeded, too. Admit it.

'So that is the story of my marriage which really wasn't, Celia, and in conclusion I wish to make a point. I have said I was in love with Denise. No matter how many poems are written about it I personally discovered that when I was denied the natural culmination to being in love there was no other plane on which I could still live with my "wife." I found she bored me, annoyed me and had many irritating habits. She was almost too sweet and understanding when all I wanted was a blazing row.'

He smiled at her. 'That is why I had to know I liked you before I loved you, Celia; why, seeing you in your home, attending a child, I was enchanted long before I dared think of asking you to marry me. When I knew I had to speak, when it became impossible to see another man taking liberties with you without feeling it as a personal affront, instead of your own private business, which it was, then I trembled more than you will ever know. Having made such a mistake as I did, having been through such a hell of unhappiness, I know how flimsy human relationships can be. I have yet to know they

171

can be strong and enduring as steel. I have to learn. You must have patience with me.'

She sighed in the crook of his arm.

'Poor Alan! I'll never let you down.'

'I'm sure you won't.' He kissed the tip of her nose. 'And I'm not going to let you down by gorging on you as though you won't still be there next week, you adorable thing. There's to be no baby for at least another year. Do you understand?'

'Yes sir,' she answered demurely. 'No baby.'

'And you must tell me if Denise ever comes again. She may be curious to find out what mischief she achieved.'

'I shall hand her her broomstick and suggest she rides out again. But in a way I'm sorry for her. She's really only half a woman.'

'She's not particularly inconvenienced. If you never desire a thing you simply don't miss it. She's a damned good doctor and should never have involved herself intimately with the emotions of others. However, all that is past history now. I would also like to know if you see this Crawley fellow at any time, providing you don't mind. He doesn't know you're married, does he? He's bound to seek you out.'

'I'll tell you,' Celia promised, biting back a little smile. 'I'll tell you absolutely everything. You can read my diary if you like.'

172

'Now you're teasing me.'

He entered into this relaxed mood and hugged her tightly, until there was one of those moments of awareness and a sudden veiling of the eyes.

'I think we ought to go to the *fiesta*, don't you, darling?'

'If you like. I'll change my dress. This one is crumpled, thanks to you.'

'I'll crumple more than your dress, my lady, if you're not ready in ten minutes stat!'

* * *

The rest of the honeymoon slipped away all too quickly, for now Celia felt she was really only just beginning to know Alan and that loving him had been very much easier. He was a complex person and yet in some respects peculiarly uncomplicated. He apparently had the power of separating himself so that the Alan who romped with her through the flowering vineyards above the villa might never even have known the distinguished back-room boy of a famous university. She never caught any sight of either the doctor or scholar the whole time they were in Spain. He was on holiday and nobody was going to distract him from the enjoyment and appreciation of every minute, and his pretty young wife could find no complaint that she was ever neglected until one day in the middle of the third week when he asked her if she would like to do some shopping in Malaga.

'Shopping?' she wrinkled her brow. The days were really warm now, and the sun a reliable friend. In a month or two it would burn and blister, but just at present it was a kiss of pure benevolence and health. 'I don't think so. I can live a little longer without shops.'

'Oh, well,' he said with a shrug, 'I expect you can find plenty to do—or not do—until I get back.'

It was a shock to her to discover that he was quite prepared to leave her and go into Malaga alone. Allowing for the two-hour journey each way he might be expected to be gone for six hours at least, and he had not attempted to persuade her to change her mind and accompany him.

She felt surprised and hurt to think that already he could face the prospect of being away from her for six hours, after all they had been to one another. He was whistling quietly as he made his preparations, and her voice was decidedly cool as she replied to his asking if he could get her anything in the city.

'No, thanks.'

She would have liked to have turned away as he stooped to kiss her, but he was so apparently unaware of having hurt her that she concluded the affliction was something

174

peculiar to her which she must investigate at leisure when he had gone.

'What'll you do?' he asked from the front porch.

She would have liked to have answered, 'Come with you, of course,' but pride was constricting her throat.

'Oh, I don't know. I expect I shall walk down to the beach later.'

'Good! I'll look out for you. You're not to go swimming, now.'

She shook her head. He had already told her that the portion of beach they overlooked was not safe for bathing. Not only was it serrated by sharks' teeth rocks but where the river emptied there were dangerous cold currents.

She did not watch him drive off, but when he had gone she enjoyed a short, sharp, relieving cry.

'Denise was r-right,' she told her sodden handkerchief, 'man's love—especially his—is a thing apart. He can turn it off at will. I wish I could. I'm a fool.'

After a solitary lunch she walked down to the beach to sunbathe. It took her half an hour, and she was relieved to strip down to her swim-suit and stretch out on a towel to cool off. There was a delicious scent of old seaweed and the sand was fine like that which runs through egg-timers. After a little while she began to see how foolish she had been for taking offence with Alan. He had, after all, asked if she wanted to go out and she had refused. To expect him not to go himself was perhaps straining the relationship beyond its endurance. People may enjoy being together, but if they were handcuffed for life they would probably hate each other before a week had passed and be unable to see the familiar and inescapable countenance without thoughts of murder in their hearts.

She baked gently on both sides and read a paperback novel she had found in the villa without real interest. It was much more absorbing to look around one on a Spanish beach. Cars flashed by on the coastal road and clearly she could see a boy and two donkeys climbing the road to Torre Nueva. Further along the beach a couple of Spaniards occupied themselves in the rock pools. Maybe there were crabs or shrimps, for they had nets and buckets, and their conversation was staccato and masculinely brief. After a while only two sombreros could be seen behind a rock and the beach lay quiet in the hour of siesta.

When Celia awoke she felt a little sore on her thighs. She hadn't meant to sleep in the sun, because she knew how dangerous this could be, but she thought at this time of year she might escape serious sunburn. She walked idly to the water's edge and sat down in the surf, allowing the salt water to break over her thighs painfully but with a healing touch. It was a pity one couldn't bathe, and yet if one could sit like this in the shallows why not go in a little deeper and get really cool? The sea looked milky and innocent, though the water was colder than she had thought possible. She looked around and saw the two sombreros still behind the rock like twin mushrooms. There was really nobody on the beach at all, only herself and the shining, tempting sea.

One step, two, and the unseen beach shelved so precipitately that the sea received her before she was quite ready and she floundered underwater, opening surprised eyes in a marine-green world before she broke surface and, treading water, laughed in the joy of the forbidden pursuit. She had once swum regularly and quite strongly, but the demands of medicine had curtailed most of her activities and now she found she was tired after just a few strokes, and not only tired but unable even to maintain her position. Though she was swimming towards the beach she was going out further and further and, kicking her legs with a renewed and desperate effort, she found one of those subterranean rocks and cried out in fear and agony as the skin was ripped from her shin. Then it was all confusion as she felt herself carried away as though by someone else's will, and her own efforts were as puny as those of a fly in a web and her fate, apparently, as inevitable.

★   ★   ★

From under his sombrero Pablo said, 'The señora is in the water.'

'*Mi madre,*' Pepe grunted. 'These foreigners are always making nuisances of themselves in siesta time. Why can't they drown themselves in working hours?'

But both brothers stood up and surveyed Celia's progress with some interest. The current curved in a wide arc, dark grey water clearly drawn through the clean green, and they knew that at one point the dark water almost beached before shooting off seawards again. Here they waited, trousers rolled up above the knee, ready to grab the brand from the burning or, more correctly, the drowning from the deep, for neither man could swim a stroke and yet they knew their stretch of coast with a respectful intimacy and had watched others fall for the blandishments of some unseen siren which apparently called the unwitting to a watery doom.

Pepe grabbed the inanimate figure as it came within reach and Pablo beached her, expertly pumping her arms and squeezing her ribs to eject sea-water. When she sighed and opened her eyes Pablo told his brother that this was the señora from the Villa Mañana where their sister Carmela was the maid.

'Then we had better take her home,' Pepe said proprietorially, and hoisted Celia up in his brown arms while Pablo went to collect the towel and beach-bag he found lying around.

'Better wrap her in this,' he suggested, offering the towel. 'If you meet Juanita carrying a woman in that state there'll be no wedding at Whitsuntide for you, brother!'

★   ★   ★

Alan had found Malaga surprisingly dull on this particular day and knew he was missing Celia more than he cared to admit. The car had needed some attention, however, and he did not care to think of the possibility of being stranded miles from anywhere, thanks to a mechanical fault, or missing the home-bound plane because of it. Better to be safe than sorry—still, he was glad when the mechanics assured him there wasn't much to be done and an hour would see the vehicle fully roadworthy once again.

He wandered idly down the broad tree-lined avenue in the centre of the city thinking what a short time it took to stop feeling bachelor-minded. Now he wanted to say 'Look at that!' or 'Listen to this!' to the woman who was his true mate. It was rather pathetic to discover one was really only half a person until in a miraculous welding one became whole and the discovery and the knowledge were an intimate secret shared, even though the whole world knew the facts.

He turned into the shopping centre, open again after the long Easter holiday, and paused to watch a dark-eyed damsel dressing a window.

Why shouldn't he buy Celia a nightie? She was his wife and he would be pleased to tell the assistant so.

Before he left the dark interior several of the assistants were in stitches of delight and he, too, was smiling. His Spanish was not brilliant, but his mime proved most entertaining. There was a frothy piece of pink nonsense in a striped bag under his arm and a song on his lips. The hour's wait was nearly up. He spent another fifty pesetas on a bunch of orange-blossom and went off to collect the car.

The drive back seemed shorter than the outward bound journey because he was returning to Celia. It was wonderful to belong to someone like this, to feel their pull when one was miles away. Approaching a blind corner near a rocky bluff, he had a sudden premonition that something big and lethal was about to meet him head on. He pulled the car well over to the right and slowed down, narrowing his eyes to meet whatever menaced, for Spanish drivers are notorious for hugging the middle of the road even when in charge of pantechnicons. The road opened out before his eyes clear and uncluttered, however, and he gazed along it in surprise. So real had been the presage of disaster that it had hit him like a blow in the face. The feeling passed, however, and his heart grew lighter again as he reached familiar territory. The stretch of beach was deserted where Celia had told him she might be. Ah, well. She would be at the villa, bless her, and he couldn't get there quickly enough.

On the steep road just short of the villa, he came upon a strange little procession. There were two brown young men, one carrying a bundle in a large towel, trailed by a long-haired wild bitch and two gangling pups. The second man was tossing bread to the hungry dam and as Alan eased the car alongside the party he saw a bare foot protruding from the towel.

All at once, as though he had been told, he knew exactly what was afoot and who it was in the towel. He was out of the car like one possessed.

'What's happened to my wife?'

Pablo glanced at his brother.

'Is this the señor?' he asked.

'I don't know. I suppose it must be. What's he saying?'

'How do I know? Fool! He looks as though he's going to hit me. I wish these foreigners would speak a civilised language instead of

181

gargling in their throats.'

Carmela came running from the villa to act as interpreter.

'Oh, señor, my brothers say the señora was in the sea. They fished her out and—' she mimed artificial respiration—'now she breathes again, but is very tired.'

Celia stirred in the towel. The journey had had a narcotic effect upon her and most of the time she had dozed. She knew, as a doctor, that this was all part of shock and that she was doing herself no harm by lying passively in her rescuer's arms and allowing nature to take its course. When she heard Alan's voice, however, she made an effort to return to normality.

'I'm all right,' she insisted. 'Please put me down, now. I'm really all right.'

Her limbs failed her, however, and she was put to bed and dosed with brandy while Pablo and Pepe were being regaled in the kitchen.

'Go to sleep now,' Alan told her kindly, as a doctor, 'I'll speak to you later,' the husband couldn't resist adding before he departed, and Celia trembled in sweet anticipation. He would be angry; of course he would, and she deserved it, but his concern and agitation had more than compensated her for her terrifying experience. A clean, cool bandage bound her skinned leg and life was doubly precious since she had almost lost it and been spared to see Alan's eyes loving her again.

CHAPTER THIRTEEN

That particular escapade did merit a very serious discussion once relief had subsided somewhat and Celia was herself again.

'I know you have been on your own a long time, Celia, and that normally you're a responsible adult. You must, however, realise that you're my responsibility now. I don't intend to interfere with the way you run the house, or your working life, but if I see fit to say something must not be done, then I expect to be obeyed. Obviously I had a good reason for saying no swimming in that particular cove, and I still shudder when I think what might have been under that towel. You must promise to heed me in future, Celia. I will never tell you not to do a thing merely to assert myself; it will be because there's good reason. Well?'

His dark eyes had, temporarily, turned into steel. That 'Well?' was almost imperious and yet she knew he was still treading uncertainly with her, getting to know her better in spite of all the joy they had known together.

'Very well, Alan, I promise. I'm sorry I disobeyed you in this matter. I was wrong and I paid for it.'

'You always will, my dear, and so, inevitably, will I.'

She said no more, for there was nothing to be said. It was sweet to be cherished, to belong, and she had no desire to break away or rebel against a discipline she knew was intended only for her good.

They returned to England to find the garden at Mildhaven drenched in lilacs and filled with their scent. It was so mild and warm for the time of year that they did not immediately miss the climate of Southern Spain and revelled in having a week's idling still ahead of them.

Neither of them idled, exactly, however. There were crates of books and papers awaiting Alan's attention. Now that he, too, was to live in the house he had to have his own study and places to keep his things. Celia had kept cupboards awaiting him and occupied herself one day unpacking textbooks for him.

'My dear, no!' he said rather sharply, coming upon her. 'I'll see to all that. I have my own weird and wonderful filing system,' he said more gently, 'but thanks all the same.'

She felt hurt at the time, but soon forgot the incident. They had so much to learn about one another that there was bound to be a little stepping on one another's toes occasionally.

Celia had heard Alan tell the daily woman and Mrs Borridge that he would do any dusting and sweeping necessary in the study

184

himself. He was intending to buy a special lock and key for the room so as to keep the children out when they were in a mood to explore.

'I have valuable papers there,' he told Celia, 'and I don't want anybody messing them about.'

Celia and the other women took to referring jokingly to the study as the 'holy of holies,' and one day, when Alan was out walking on the common with the children, a swivel chair was delivered to the house. It was not new, but it looked comfortable and had apparently just been re-upholstered. Obviously it would be at home nowhere else but in the study.

'In here, please,' Celia directed the men, opening the door of the sanctum.

It was not the first time she had been in the study, of course, neither did she feel herself bound by any veto to keep out. She had not been in the room since Alan had taken possession, however, and once the men had left she looked around with interest. There was a photograph of Alan's mother on the desk and an old snapshot of his father, a gentle-looking giant of a man with a fine moustache topping a small, clipped beard.

'I bet Alan would look like that with a beard!' Celia cried out in delight. 'I'll ask him to grow one.'

She replaced the snapshot and began

automatically to tidy papers on the cluttered desk. A warning note in her brain told her that she shouldn't do this, and it was at this moment she heard the children's voices as they returned from their walk.

In hastening to greet them she knocked over a cardboard carton containing manuscript and the pages flew like birds all over the brown carpet.

'Oh, goodness!' she gasped.

The pages were not numbered and she could make no sense of the technical hieroglyphics involved. She glanced up from the carpet, looking and feeling extremely guilty, to meet Alan's dark, accusing stare.

'I'm sorry,' she said quickly, 'I knocked this over and—and I'm afraid your papers are all mixed up.'

He snatched the pages from her and surveyed them silently for a moment as though mentally counting up to ten.

'I thought I made it clear that I would do anything that was necessary in here?' he breathed through an atmosphere thick as a fog.

'Yes, well,' she replied, 'your chair arrived, so I asked the men to put it in here.'

He gazed around in annoyance.

'You mean you allowed workmen to trample about in here?'

'Why not?' she suddenly flashed back at him. 'I supervised the whole operation and they didn't take anything. Anyway, what is there to take, apart from rubbishy old papers which would only interest cranks like yourself?'

He looked down at her as though she was a bad smell coming under the door.

'If you've quite finished behaving like a fishwife perhaps you will respect my wishes in future and keep out of my study?'

She blazed up like a beacon.

'I'll keep out, don't worry. I don't know what you imagine is so attractive about being in here at all, but it certainly isn't present company.' She felt tears trembling behind her eyelids and made her escape before he should see her dissolving into feminine weakness.

She heard his voice calling 'Celia! Celia, don't be silly. Come back!'

She disregarded this, however, and hid in the linen closet to indulge in a weep and investigate her hurt unobserved. Fortunately Mrs Borridge was shopping in the village and Mrs Fern was in her own quarters, so the little contretemps had been quite private. Even the children were still playing in the garden, loth to come indoors on such a lovely day.

Celia heard Alan come upstairs and go into the bedroom calling 'Celia!' in a rather constrained way. After a while she heard the stairs creak again and gave a long, quivering sigh. She wished she need never come out of the cupboard to be hurt so again.

Alan, deciding she must be upstairs somewhere, finally ran her down.

'Whatever are you doing in here?' he asked.

'Packing towels,' she said quickly. 'At least I have a right to be here.'

'I'm sorry,' he said suddenly, disarmingly. 'You have a right to be anywhere you wish. I was wrong. I was stupid. Please forgive me.'

'Of c-course I forgive you,' she said stiffly, 'but I shall never feel happy in the study again.'

'I'm a pig to make you unhappy.' He took her suddenly into his arms and the tears readily returned so that they dampened his shirt and his lips as he tried to stem them with kisses. 'Don't cry, Celia. It hurts my heart to see you cry and to think I did it. I suppose we had to have a tiff one day, but say you forgive me. Do say it.'

'There's really nothing to forgive. I was noseying round your study or it wouldn't have happened.'

'Please nose whenever you like.'

'No. You have a right to your privacy and your work's important. I—I didn't mean what I said about cranks.'

'I rather hoped you did,' he said with a smile. 'It shook me up and I expect did my conceit quite a lot of good. Call me a crank whenever I behave like one, will you?'

She had to laugh, even through her tears. In retrospect it all did seem rather absurd.

'Very well,' she agreed. 'And you must tell me when I'm a fishwife again.'

They looked at each other mutely for a moment as though amazed that such things had been said and hurt so much.

Finally there was another long kiss and all was over, the day bright and shining again.

'I'll make the tea,' Celia decided. 'It will be nice for Mrs Borridge to come in to.'

In the kitchen, her own large, shiny modern kitchen, she felt more like a married woman than she had felt in all these weeks because there was a little pain tucked away among all the ecstasy. She also knew, in her heart, that honeymoons always have to come to an end and marriage must learn to stand on its workaday feet. She sighed as she thought it, but cheered up quickly. Whoever heard of a young woman on honeymoon cutting sandwiches so thinly and daintily, spreading butter thickly and ham and cucumber generously so as to please her husband? And yet there was a very real pleasure in such simple pursuits, and these could go on and on ad infinitum. Oh, yes, there was much more to marriage than the honeymoon, and only a fool would baulk at stepping out adventurously down the unknown paths of the future.

It seemed strange to be going back to work again as a married woman. After a cup of early morning tea, Alan was up first and taking his bath while Celia dallied and only thought about it. In Harley Street she started work later than her husband in his research job, but they made a habit of having breakfast together with Fiona, who was very lively at this early hour of the day and full of amusing chatter. Now that there was so much garden, and such a large house, she was asking for a puppy. In an area where the canine breed almost matched the human population in numbers, this was only natural. Whenever the children were taken out they saw people exercising or playing with dogs. To own a dog had become an obsession with Fiona and, childlike, she introduced the subject on every possible occasion.

On this morning, merely playing with her cereal, she prattled, 'Me and Billy know—'

'Billy and I,' Celia automatically corrected.

'Oh, do you and Billy want a dog, too?' the child asked delightedly. 'I fought he wanted to share wif me. That means we can have two doggies . . .'

Alan choked into his coffee and Celia frowned reprovingly. She felt he encouraged Fiona to chatter so that he could report her funny little sayings to his fellow scientists.

'No, Fiona,' she explained. 'You said that wrongly. You must always say, "Billy and I," not "me and Billy." Now do you understand?'

'Oh. Well, Billy and—and I know what sort of a doggie we want. We've fought about it a lot. We would like a lovely little false terrier.'

This time there was no holding Alan. He slapped his thigh in absolute glee and repeated it over and over again.

'A false terrier! By Jove, that's good! Wait till I tell that to John. His boy wrote an essay describing some historical character who was hanged, drawn and *halved*. But this beats the lot. Well, goodbye for now, my fair ladies.' He kissed Fiona on the nose and rumpled her hair. Celia he kissed full on the lips and gave her a meaning look. 'See you both anon.'

Fiona asked. 'Was I funny again, Aunty C.?'

'You didn't mean to be, darling, but it was funny, really. You meant fox terrier and you said false, which means something else altogether. You don't mind when we laugh at you, do you?'

'No. I like making Uncle Alan laugh. Why don't you make him laugh, Aunty?'

'Well, people can't be laughing all the time. It's something that's nice to do once in a while.'

'Will I get my—what you said—terrier?'

Celia hesitated to give a direct answer. Next week the question of the child's custody was being heard in court. Anything might happen, even though one prayed hard for things to be allowed to go on as they were.

'If you want a dog, Fiona, you must earn it by being good and then, perhaps, on your birthday . . .' By July they should all know where they stood.

'Is that a long time?'

'Not really. The puppy you're going to have may just be getting born now. But he's got to stay with his mother until he's old enough to eat biscuits. You can wait that long, can't you?'

'I think so,' Fiona said uncertainly. 'Oh, look! I didn't finish my breakfast, and here's Billy all ready for kiddygarten.'

The two children had been attending a kindergarten school in the mornings for a couple of weeks and thoroughly enjoyed it.

'And I must rush,' Celia decided. 'You must be a good girl and eat, Fiona. You're a mere scrap alongside Billy. Have a lovely day, darling.'

There was an easy tenor about those late spring days. Besides all the interest of work there was a renewed interest in going home each evening. Fiona looked forward to the evening hour when she could tell her guardians of the highlights of her days; how Billy had pushed her off the swing and she had retaliated by hitting him with her toy broom; how another girl at kiddygarten had a new baby brother and teacher had said 'How nice if we could all have one!'

'So can we?' she concluded this particular episode.

Celia glanced at Alan who smiled significantly.

'One thing at a time,' he told the child. 'When you get your dog he won't want a baby hogging all the attention. He would be jealous.'

That evening Alan bathed Fiona, and Celia could hear them chatting fifty to the dozen. It was funny how, when one was married, one thought a great deal about babies. It was as though some natural force was at work keeping one's thoughts directed towards this end. One looked at other people's babies with a new interest and baby-linen shops were suddenly as attractive to a woman as jewellers. Celia, at unoccupied moments of her days, tried out names experimentally. Regretfully she had to drop her favourite 'Georgiana,' as, when attached to Grainger, it had the effect on the tongue of a cement-crusher. She thought the classical favourites, Elizabeth, Mary, Anne and Jane all sounded lovely, as did apostolic names for a boy. She had no idea about Alan's preferences and asked him one evening before getting into bed.

'Names?' he asked, squinting at her thoughtfully. 'Plain and wholesome like home cooking. What d'you want a name for?'

'Our child, when we have one.'

He caught hold of her without more ado, half undressed as she was.

'You never let go, do you? A real dainty little bull—whatever they call lady dogs.'

'A doctor, and so squeamish!' she teased.

He bit her ear gently so that she let out a squeal.

'Membership—baby, in that order, madam,' he said inexorably, 'and to prove I can resist your charms I shall sleep in my dressing room.'

She gazed after him ruefully until, in the doorway, he paused and winked broadly.

'I have to get up at six, early start,' he explained, 'and I don't want to disturb my sweet wife. Goodnight, darling.'

'Goodnight, Alan.'

She felt lonely slipping into the big bed for the first time alone.

How quickly one adjusted to married life! Such a short while ago the thing which would most have worried her, in a contemplated union, would have been the thought of losing the privacy of her bedroom.

As she snuggled down she wondered about Alan's early start. He had mentioned being 'on to something big,' but she didn't really understand a great deal about his work.

Perhaps she was guilty of not showing enough interest, but when they talked she always remembered that sickening exhibition they had attended together with the terrible pictures, and so was glad to change the subject.

'I hope I don't become too jealous of his work,' she thought sleepily, 'that it doesn't intrude too much into our private lives.'

But had she known her husband better, she would have realised that such a man never counts the cost where his life's dream is concerned, nor does he ask his wife's permission to be allowed to make his dream a workable reality.

This Celia still had to find out the hard way, from personal experience.

CHAPTER FOURTEEN

The court-room was hot and the windows so high up in the panelled walls that the place seemed to be airless with smells of old polished leather and dusty books and a faint tang from the panelling itself, as though it had recently been treated for woodworm.

The case for the custody of Fiona Isabelle Derwent, three years and ten months old, was called: Grainger versus Wicheter. Celia had never met the Wicheters previously and had a vague idea of the way she expected them to look from their letters. She couldn't have been more wrong. She had imagined Mr Wicheter to be an elderly type of cowboy, long, lean and desiccated with a skin of yellow leather and a ten-gallon hat; Mrs Wicheter had been tiny, motherly and white-haired, always attired in a large white apron over a plain, voluminous black dress.

The couple who came forward to sit at the large table, with their lawyer and a barrister, however, might have been any London couple walking into the court out of the nearby street. Mr Wicheter was tall and had a plump, rather stern face. He looked a typical company director, with pale, assessing eyes. Mrs Wicheter's hair must certainly have been white by nature, but it was at the moment pale lavender and exquisitely coiffured. She wore a suit of silk jersey and looked slim, assured, excellently corseted and confident.

Celia's confidence had taken a dip, and Alan nudged her and said 'Buck up!' before the judge's gavel brought everybody to attention.

'Let us hope this case can be decided without acrimony from either side,' the great man said clearly, thus making an oblique reference to the previous case where divorced parents had played a bitter tug-of-war with their only offspring, a frightened and confused little boy. 'We are here to decide what is best for the child in the case and not who can win over the other. A human being is not for winning. A child is a serious charge and a temporary one. Any child grows up and leaves the nest eventually. But the fledgling is shaped in the nest, and when the Court is asked to make a decision it is always a serious one in a case like this. Now, can you state the case for your clients, Mr Demarest?'

Both cases were presented by Counsel mainly giving the facts, that the Wicheters had adopted the child's mother and brought her up as their own daughter and wished to do the same for Fiona, regarding her as their grandchild. How she would be well educated, personally supervised and brought up in a wonderful climate with opportunities for travel now that the claimants were retired from active work on their sheep-station.

For the Graingers it was said that the child's aunt, then Dr Celia Derwent, had taken the little girl into her care after she was discharged from the hospital where her parents had been taken in a moribund state after being involved in a road accident. Dr Derwent had reorganised her working life to give herself more time to spend with her niece; she was employed in exclusive practice as an assistant to a specialist and therefore had regular hours and a guaranteed time off duty including all weekends. At first she had occupied the flat which had been the child's parents' home, but now that Dr Derwent had married the family had moved out into the country where the little one had a large garden and a little playmate living in the same house. The child had settled down very well with her aunt and new uncle, Mr Bluff said in conclusion, and was very happy with the added advantage of having two doctors in the family to look after her health.

'Oh, I don't know about that, m'dear fellow,' said Mr Justice Wandsworth, lugubriously. 'If the cobbler's child is the worst-shod I'm sure a doctor's tots are much more likely to have their aches and pains dismissed as imagination than the little dears brought to the surgery. Let's not get carried away. Dr and Mrs Grainger are here as prospective foster-parents, not as a couple of paediatricians.'

There were polite smiles all round, and Celia hated it. She couldn't see anything to laugh about in the present situation.

Later Counsel were invited to ask questions of the opposition. It was all done in a friendly fashion and was most informal, but there was a deadly purpose behind everything and Celia's heart dropped like a stone when Mr Demarest, the Wicheters' Counsel, suddenly addressed her in his well-bred, disarming voice.

'Dr Derwent, as I believe you are still known professionally . . .' she nodded nervously, 'you have been married a little over a month, I gather?'

'That is so.'

'You married Professor Grainger, yet I believe as recently as last September you were planning to marry somebody else? A Dr Marquess—your husband's half-brother?'

There was an expectant hush.

'No. I never really intended to marry Dr Marquess, who is now deceased.'

'But you wrote a letter saying that you did,' Mr Demarest proceeded inexorably. 'You caused the information to be passed on to my clients as a—forgive the expression—a spoke in your wheel.'

Celia wanted to creep under the table and die, but instead gritted her teeth to reply.

'I think any proposal of marriage is inclined to go to a woman's head, sir,' she explained. 'Dr Marquess was famous, handsome, wealthy and I liked him. I was flattered and, yes, I could see such a match strengthening my claim to keep Fiona, and so I wrote that letter. But when I realised I was not in love with Dr Marquess I couldn't go through with such a marriage, not even for Fiona. My lawyer no doubt informed you of my change of mind?'

'Yes, he did. I take it there was no intent to deceive on your part?'

'None whatsoever.'

'And your marriage is not merely contrived

to strengthen your claim to the custody of your niece?'

'It is not,' Celia almost blazed. 'Our marriage was hastened for convenience' sake, but I was in love with my husband then as I am now!'

She bit her lip as she realised what she had just tossed out for everyone's delectation. She had never actually told Alan how she felt about him, and now she had shouted it out in court, angrily, and his head was bowed and tense as he tapped the table in front of him.

'That will be all, Dr Derwent,' smiled the barrister, and the Wicheters smiled at one another and whispered together.

The judge began to assess in a monotonous experienced voice, explaining that it was not his way to play Solomon and suggest chopping a child in half. He had seen the little girl, he said, and she was a normal, happy, intelligent little thing. He thought the idea of an upbringing in New South Wales was excellent; all young people would benefit from the outdoor life and sunny climate; but if every child was lured away by these inducements it would be as sad a day for Britain as it had been for Hamelin when the youngsters went the way of the rats. Britain wasn't such a bad place for children and its spring was second to none in the world. On the rare occasions when we had a good summer this island of ours would take some beating, and why was it so many Australians came for a visit and made up their minds to stay? It was a decidedly two-way traffic.

Celia's spirits began to climb.

'My sympathies go out to Mr and Mrs Wicheter, however,' the judge proceeded. 'They have lost their adopted daughter tragically and have never seen her child until today when they met in my chambers. If I do not grant them custody it is unlikely they will ever get to know the child, for it is not as though they live just around the corner and can be granted reasonable access to her. One may also presume that Professor and Mrs Grainger will eventually have children of their own, something apparently denied the older claimants who have already lavished love and affection on an adopted child.'

Celia's spirits dropped again.

'Yet one does not expect the mother of a large family to share out her offspring among the childless. This little girl we are discussing is, to all intents and purposes, the first child of this new marriage. She has been brought through a dark period of her young life without a scar because of the love and understanding lavished upon her by her deceased father's only sister. My conclusions mainly rest with Professor Grainger's attitude towards this child. I have studied his replies to Counsel and find him a worthy stand-in for the child's father. I have no hesitation in granting custody to the Graingers, with certain qualifications.

'I suggest,' he went on, 'that as the Wicheters are prepared to stay in England for the summer they be allowed reasonable access to the child for the duration so that they get to know her and she them. Thereafter, once she is old enough to travel, perhaps she could fly to New South Wales for the long summer holidays? It is better to use this double claim to the child's advantage than otherwise. That is as I decide, ladies and gentlemen, and I trust it will prove an amicable arrangement.'

Celia could scarcely believe that it was over and Fiona was now really hers, hers and Alan's, to bring up without the threat of the past months hanging over their heads like the sword of Damocles.

Outside the court the Wicheters were waiting, looking a little down in the mouth. Alan went up to them with his hand outstretched and soon there were smiles again as they planned what was to be done next.

'I'm fixing them up at the George,' Alan said as they stood waiting for a taxi to take them to the station and home. 'From there they can do all the sightseeing they require and pop in to Mildhaven whenever they want.'

'Need you have been quite so eager to start this business off?' Celia asked. 'We're obviously going to see enough of them this summer without rushing things.'

Alan looked at her but said nothing. Mrs Borridge was sitting opposite with a decidedly fidgety Fiona on her lap. The small girl had soon tired of the confines of the court ante-room where she had been required to stay pending other people's pleasure for far too long. She wanted to get back home to Billy as soon as possible.

'Why didn't we go to the Zoo?' she now demanded as she was hustled on to the station platform where the Aylesbury train was already standing and filling rapidly, it being the rush hour.

'Never mind, my sweet,' Alan said indulgently. 'It hasn't been a very nice day for you, but you'll never know!' He sighed and gave her a quick hug. 'We'll make the Zoo another day and you can play outside when we get home.'

'Are you joking?' Celia asked from her seat in the corner. 'It will be her bedtime when we get back, and she'd better learn life isn't all trips to the Zoo.'

Alan again didn't respond, but his lips were tight, and when the party was at last home and Mrs Borridge making an uplifting cup of tea, he called Celia into his study. He had already dismissed Fiona into the garden, despite his wife's protests, insisting that the loss of half an hour's sleep was neither here nor there after an extraordinary day.

'Firstly,' he said, pouring out two glasses of sherry, 'I think we both need this rather more than tea. There were some bad moments this afternoon.'

'I think on the whole you came through it rather well,' Celia remembered. 'The judge practically said he was handing Fiona over because he liked you. He didn't think nearly so much of me. Of course I allowed that awful, smarmy Demarest man to rattle me . . .'

'You did become rather over-emotional, I think.'

She was nettled.

'Telling the whole world I was in love with you, you mean? I should have known better, been calm, cool and unemotional like you were, I suppose?'

'A little self-control doesn't necessarily mean one is lacking in emotion, Celia.'

'But that's what you meant, isn't it?' her eyes were blazing and she was ready for anything, a lovely stranger to his critical sight. In this guise he felt he didn't know her at all.

'If you're determined to row, Celia, may I get my complaint in? I don't like to be deflated in front of other people, nor have my instructions countermanded by you in similar circumstances. You can criticise my actions as much as you like in private. Not only did your remark about my hastiness in fixing up the Wicheters annoy me, it also embarrassed Mrs Borridge. Also Fiona can't respect two adults who descend to arguing about her bedtime in public. Rules are something else which can be fixed in private, or, if one relaxes them, explanations and reproofs can be administered similarly. I hope I make myself clear?'

'Very clear,' Celia said in tones of ice. 'I gather that there is only one rule-maker in this house, and this is his private sanctum? Now that I've been put in my place yet once again, I take it I can go?'

'Oh, Celia, don't let's be childish!' he begged.

'Don't let me be childish, you really mean. You never consider you can be in the wrong, do you? You never think that you can be overbearing and pompous? Well, you are. Both, and often.'

He said, 'Have you finished?'

'No, I haven't. Not by a long chalk.'

'Then can we continue when you're a little calmer? I'm sure your shouting can be heard in the kitchen.'

As she breathed hard and made no attempt to move he excused himself and left the study. She could hear him calling Fiona and, a little later, the nursery bath tap running.

She carried her anger with her like Christian carried his burden. Tea was laid in the sitting room, but had not been touched.

Celia poured a cup and drank it, feeling no better for it. She then marched upstairs and into Fiona'a bathroom where the child was splashing surrounded by plastic ducks and small boats. Alan was wearing the plastic apron which always hung behind the bathroom door.

'Do you mind if I take over my own job now?' she asked. She usually bathed Fiona, although Alan did it sometimes for a treat.

'Not at all. Actually she's done. She just wants drying off when you're ready.'

'As it's already ages past her bedtime I'm quite ready.'

He handed her the big white towel and across it smiled placatingly and mouthed the word 'Pax?'

'Thank you.' She couldn't warm up one syllable. She turned her back on him and hauled Fiona, protesting, out of the cluttered bath. When she heard the door shut behind her she knew the olive branch had gone along with Alan and that he was not a man to turn the other cheek too often with a slap as his only reward. She felt miserable, suddenly, her anger dissolving and leaving only the guilty conviction that she was in the wrong all along the line. Was she such a paragon of all the virtues that she could not bear to be thought fallible on any account? Of course she should not have criticised Alan for making overtures to the Wicheters she would have found so difficult to make herself, and to involve Mrs Borridge as a witness to her disapproval was equally unforgivable. Alan had not said, 'Don't criticise me,' he had said 'Don't criticise me in public,' which was, of course, a reasonable enough request to make of anyone. But she, discovering an ill-natured and unreasonable side to her own character, had merely taken offence after offence and howled him down. Lastly, she, who was in the wrong, had snubbed his overtures of friendship, he who was in the right and had kept himself under control at all times.

'Aunty Celia,' came Fiona's voice into her unhappy thoughts, 'I like Uncle Alan. Why don't you?'

'Oh, but I do, darling.' She bit her lip as she realised how sensitive both animals and the very young are to 'atmosphere'. She must have brought an unhappy aura, as thick as a fog, into the room with her. 'We're all a bit tired after today,' she explained awkwardly. We'll feel better in the morning.'

'Can Uncle Alan bath me tomorrow?'

'Yes, if you would like him to.'

But the next day Alan did not come home at all. He had his *pied-à-terre*, of course, his flat in town, still functioning, and after telephoning that he would be working very late he suggested it might be better to sleep there. As he had slept the previous night in his dressing room, after a *tête-à-tête* dinner

207

during which they might have been two strangers sharing a table in a restaurant because there was no other place to go, she felt that he was demonstrating his preference for his own company still and felt very unhappy and uncertain.

How tenuous was a marriage founded on physical attraction, after all! Really the physical was all they had in common, despite Alan's abhorrence of such a situation. He kept trying to establish other planes on which they could meet, but she knew she was heavy going. She wanted him to love her all the time, needed his arms around her as though in reassurance that he found her desirable above all. Perhaps it was true that women placed too much importance on sexual relationships so that the accusation, 'You don't love me any more,' really meant 'You don't desire me any more,' and in that denial stupid women allowed their hearts to ache and break.

Celia spent a terrible day and had a patient whose collective symptoms resisted her powers of diagnosis, ill-disposed as she was to give the matter her undivided attention. She eventually called in Dr Wilkes-Mather, who beckoned her aside for a conference.

'A glaring case of myxoedema, Celia,' he said teasingly. 'What's the matter with you? I would have thought the honeymoon would have been over by now.'

208

She said, 'Of course, sir,' without further comment, and went back to tell her patient that she needed to enter a hospital for treatment.

'I'm a fool to allow my domestic problems to interfere with my work,' she told herself grimly. 'I'll bet Alan hasn't made any blunders because of me today. I must make it up with him. Why can't I admit I'm at fault and say I'm sorry like any normal woman? I never knew before that I was so pig-headed.'

But when she arrived home, ready to beg forgiveness, it was to hear that Alan had telephoned saying he would be staying in town.

A grim evening was made even more grim by the announcement of a visitor, and for the third time Denise Raven presented her beautiful dispassionate self to an uneasy Celia.

CHAPTER FIFTEEN

'My dear, I had to bring you a present.' Denise's kiss was as light and fleeting as a butterfly. Celia was surprised that it did not sting, and immediately regretted such an uncharitable thought. 'I know it's late, but it had to be something very, very special. Open it when I've gone.' She placed a tissue-wrapped parcel on the table and settled herself in a comfortable chair near the open french windows, her long, elegant legs crossed at the ankles. Her two-piece was in blue uncrushable linen. She looked elegant and beautiful, like priceless porcelain.

'Marriage hasn't done anything for you yet,' she said teasingly. 'You look as though all the cares of the world are on your young shoulders.'

'No, I have no cares,' Celia lied. 'I had a difficult case today that I'm still mulling over. I'm sorry Alan isn't in . . .'

'I know he isn't in, my dear. I had lunch with him.'

'You had—' The hurt in Celia's voice could not be disguised. She coughed quickly and reached for the sherry to pour two glasses.

'Why not?' Denise asked lightly. 'We've remained good friends. You supply one need of Alan's, I supply another. It's a most amicable arrangement. Don't you agree? Oh, thank you. Alan always keeps very good sherry.'

'This happens to be a bottle I picked up at the local off-licence, and I haven't a clue about wines,' Celia said with some asperity. 'You're welcome to a glass if you wish.'

Denise took the glass, sniffed, wrinkled her nose and sipped.

'You must ask Alan to educate you in such matters, my dear. Use the rest of this stuff for cooking. It's a bit rough, isn't it?'

'I don't think so. I must disagree with you, Dr Raven. You can have whisky if you prefer. Alan did buy that.'

'No, thank you. There's no need to sound so offended, my dear. One can always learn from others. I would be delighted to give you the benefit of my experience on any subject.'

'Such as how to stay married to Alan. I would like my marriage to last rather longer than yours did. "Till death us do part," for instance.'

Denise flushed, uncertain of the other's mood. Underneath a calm exterior Celia was blazing with indignation.

'Surely that's in your own hands, Mrs Grainger?'

'And out of yours, Dr Raven,' Celia said with deadly intent. 'I would prefer you not to come here again. You can see Alan when and where you like, but this is my home, and I don't think you're any friend of mine.'

Denise was watchful of her adversary by now. What she had thought of as a mouse had turned into a creature of fang and claw.

'I was prepared to be your friend,' she said uncertainly. 'Why otherwise would I come here?'

'In the first place to make sure I didn't give Alan what you were not prepared to give him yourself, Dr Raven. Well, that visit was entirely wasted, you'll be sorry to know. There are no grounds for the annulment of my marriage. In the second place you came to see if there was any breach which could possibly be widened between us, and here, too, you will be unsuccessful. Alan and I have tiffs, but we've meant more to one another than you will ever know. I didn't like hearing that you are still seeing him, but I'll try to be broadminded about it. If he must see you, he must. But I don't have to see you, and now I would like you to go.'

'You—you're turning me out?' Denise asked with a thin smile.

'I will, if necessary,' Celia promised, and thrust the tissued parcel back at its donor. 'This will come in handy for the next marriage you don't approve of.'

Denise almost snatched at the parcel.

'I think Alan has a problem in you, the poor dear,' she snapped.

'I think we can say he's used to those?' Celia returned. 'At least it's not the same problem.'

'I'll give this so-called marriage a year, if that.'

'I hope you can get a bookmaker to accept your bet. But don't bank on it. I wouldn't like to think of you without either money or clothes at your time of life.'

Denise glared, but could think of no retort. The front door slammed and the big Jensen drove away with an angry roar of its exhaust.

Celia stood, her breast still rising and

falling from the encounter, and then she realised what she had actually done and put her hand to her head in horror.

When she was calmer she decided to get the business off her chest immediately. It was no good doing Denise's work for her by antagonising Alan further. She rang the number of his flat in London and eventually heard him respond.

'Alan, this is Celia.'

'Oh. Hello, Celia.'

Telephones weren't the best media for confidences at any time. They were cold, functional machines.

'I've just done something really terrible,' she blundered on. 'I almost threw your wife out of the house.'

'My wife . . . ?' he echoed.

'Oh, of course that's me, isn't it? I'm so upset I don't know what I'm saying. I had a visit from Denise, and I insulted her and told her to go and never come here again.'

'You what?'

'I know. Isn't it awful? I don't know what to do now. Should I write and apologise or—or can you suggest anything else?'

Alan was making queer little noises at the other end of the line. Could it be that he was actually chuckling?

'Alan, I can't hear you,' she said in some agitation.

'Celia, don't do anything. You chucked her

213

out? Well, let her stay chucked. Well done, you!'

'You mean that? I sort of couldn't stand her any more and lost my temper. She brought a present and I gave her that back, too. I've got an awful bad temper lately. Honestly, I didn't used to be like this, Alan. I shriek at you. I don't mean to. What can be wrong with me?'

'Growing pains, dearest.'

'What could be growing at my age?'

'Our marriage,' he said softly. 'I've got them, too. You fly off the handle and I go into a mood. I was more unhappy yesterday, after our encounter, than I care to think about, but at least I was feeling, which is better than emotional paralysis, I suppose.'

'Why didn't you come home this evening?' she asked softly. 'Is your mood still bad?'

'No. I had a lot of work to do and it's better done without distractions of any sort. I'll be home tomorrow, D.V. Did Denise tell you we lunched together?'

'She did, at the earliest opportunity.'

'I'll bet she did! Actually she turned up on the off chance at my club and the doorman, recognising her, admitted her to my table. There was no plan for us to meet.'

'If there was I still don't mind, Alan. I think she still has a kind of need of you.'

'Then it must be discouraged. You're my wife, Celia, and you're enough.'

'I bet you think I'm more than enough on occasion, Alan! Anyway, I'll leave you to get on with your work and go to my lonely bed.'

He responded fittingly, and she laughed.

'You say that from a safe distance, I notice,' she told him, her cheeks blushing pink. What he told her after that she took off to bed with her feeling reassured and happy. How tenuous was one thing, how strong another, and how complex marriage was to be sure. Her heart had been as heavy as lead all day, yet now, after a few words with the being who could strike her down with his frown, her cup of joy was again running over.

'Marriage gives one tremendous power over another person,' she thought with the wonderment of one who learns a new lesson every day, 'and power is such a precious responsibility. I wonder if I will ever know how to use my power to make Alan the happiest man in the world, seeing that that's my overriding ambition? I daren't tell him it means more to me than my Membership.'

★   ★   ★

The summer was passing, sun and shower, sweet and sour, both in life as in weather. Celia sometimes found married life so sweet that she sang little *te deums* all day long when her heart needed to express its joy or burst in her chest. Alan seemed to be happy, too, though he was, perhaps, a little too careful of showing it. He could pass from moments of rapture to sheer mundanity sometimes without a change of expression and then Celia would ask herself, 'Was this so? Did I imagine it? Why can Alan forget so easily what's been between us?'

But Alan did not forget, it was simply that Celia didn't read him yet after so brief an acquaintance as theirs had been. If there were no words her disappointment blinded her to the softness of his eyes and the serenity being with her had wrought in his mien. She wanted to be told and he was telling her, but it was in his own way and she had not yet learned to interpret this. She was often hurt and would shrink away from explanations and discussions; in this he found her moody and respected what he imagined to be a desire in her to be alone—as much as this was possible in the circumstances. At such times she would often weep because he didn't appear to care about her. They had to have time to get to know one another, and the kindest thing which could have happened to them would have been a transportation overnight to a desert island for two. But this didn't happen and, unlike most newly-weds, that summer found them hemmed in by other people so that Alan was often driven into spending nights in town. Celia was also studying hard, and she became edgier and edgier as the

Wicheters turned up at the house day after day, monopolising Fiona, plying her with gifts and sweets and, apparently, doing their level best to spoil her.

At last Celia rounded on her husband.

'They're talking of putting off their return to Australia until November. Honestly, Alan, I can't stand much more of them. Whenever I come home they're here, baby-talking to Fiona, and she plays up to them and answers in the same way. She knows perfectly well how to say "horse" and "dog," and I could have slapped her the other day when she was referring to "gee-gees" and "bow-wows." Something's got to be done or I'll blow up in front of them!'

'Calm down,' Alan suggested gently. 'I think you've got to learn a few of the facts of life, Celia. You, or rather we, were given custody of the child and the Wicheters were granted certain rights of access. Correct? Well, we've got to assert ourselves as custodians and do what is best for Fiona, no matter whose toes get stepped on. "Reasonable access," the judge said, not a total besotting. Would you allow me to handle things without a blow-up? I think it might be better for you, my dear. I don't want you to get upset.'

'What will you tell the Wicheters, Alan?'

'Just leave it to me. Have faith in me.'

Celia's spirits soared when Mrs Wicheter

informed her that they would be returning to New South Wales in about a month's time.

'How did you manage it?' Celia asked her husband admiringly. 'They seem almost glad to go.'

'They're feeling their ages, my dear,' he answered mysteriously. 'I told them we were having the decorators in and would they like to take Fiona off on various expeditions. I arranged for them to go to the Zoo and the circus. Having had Fiona to the Zoo myself, I know how inexhaustible she is and what she would do to them. I made it very clear that it wouldn't be possible to entertain them at the house for some time, but as they were primarily interested in Fiona they could have her undivided companionship for a few days. Then, I said, as she had missed so much kindergarten and would be starting real school soon, she would have to cut out all the messing about and get down to learning her lessons if she wasn't going to be a moron. I also remarked that she had been speaking perfectly good English ever since I had known her and now, for some inexplicable reason, she had retrogressed into babbling baby talk. That, I said, had got to stop, as it sounded idiotic coming from an intelligent child like her.'

'You're wonderful,' Celia said, kissing him impulsively. 'I thought you were mad when Mrs Borridge told me Fiona was going here and there with the Wicheters, but I kept my peace. I also wondered why men appeared from nowhere and took the stair-carpet up. I thought we already had a very nice staircase.'

'They're merely taking off the old varnish and putting on new. But it's a long job, and nothing looks more like an upset house than having the stair-carpet up.'

'You're a genius!' Celia grinned, and rubbed noses with him.

He grabbed her suddenly and said 'Damn!' when Mrs Fern appeared trailing Billy and Fiona home from the village.

Celia felt that he resented having people always about the place, that he was feeling the weight of Fiona and her 'entourage' more than he would admit. She fancied he brooded about things without speaking, and one evening there was one of those sudden squalls which spring up out of nowhere.

The Wicheters had left the previous Friday, it was early August, and the children were, of course, on holiday from their kindergarten. For some time they had been little imps of mischief and occasionally did very naughty things indeed. Billy, who was six months older than Fiona, periodically became bored with her now that he had got to know other boys, and perhaps he suggested activities which he knew to be naughty merely to assert his little boyhood and show off to one who hung upon his every word and action worshippingly.

On this particular Saturday morning Alan came thundering in search of Celia, who was reading up the aetiology of hypothermia and pruritus in the elderly, to refresh her memory for her Membership examinations due to take place the following month.

'Celia,' he said, finding her on the window-seat of the guest room where she was wont to retire for the peace and quiet required for her studies, 'something drastic has to be done about those children. Fiona has to be punished.'

'Oh?' She grew pale before his eyes. 'What has she done?'

'Almost burned the toolshed down. They lit a fire, using'—he almost choked—'paraffin. They might both have been killed.'

'Well, Fiona can't strike matches,' Celia immediately said defensively, 'so it must have been Billy. He's becoming a little menace.'

'Billy is at this moment getting a thundering good hiding from his mama,' Alan said, 'and our little darling supplied the matches. She sneaked them from the kitchen. What do you propose to do about it?'

'What do I propose to do? You don't suggest I beat her, do you? A child of—of four?'

'I was well beaten,' Alan said gruffly, 'and it never harmed me.'

'Well, you were a boy and probably as

naughty as Billy. But little girls—'

'They aren't sugar and spice when they do wrong, Celia. She's in her room waiting for "treatment" and she's going to get it from one or the other of us. She'll think twice about filching matches again.'

'I'll tell her it was very naughty' Celia said hastily. 'I'll make her listen to me.'

'The way you made her listen about tying Bingo's legs together so that he fell over for their infantile amusement? The way she listened when she trod in the wet varnish three times? We don't want another fire, Celia. Next time we may not be so lucky and we might have a funeral on our hands. Now don't let this matter cool any longer. Is it to be you—or I?'

Celia was by now paper-white.

'I couldn't strike her,' she whispered.

Alan's countenance spoke volumes as he looked at her and then turned on his heel without another word.

Celia listened outside the nursery, hearing Fiona say, 'Uncle Alan, what are you doing?' There followed two resounding smacks and then a surprised, anguished wail.

'Now get into bed until suppertime,' Alan's voice said sternly, 'and stop that silly row.'

Fiona's voice hiccupped into silence.

Celia was standing, her heart thudding against her ribs, as Alan came out of the nursery, a frown darkening his countenance.

'You are not to go in to her,' he said ominously.

'Oh, you—you—' she felt almost dizzy with the emotion weighing her down, the shock—'bully!' she tossed out finally. 'It's a good thing she's in your power, isn't it? You can knock her about as much as you like now that you've got a taste for it.'

His face turned a peculiar shade of grey. She was learning that this happened when he was feeling extremely angry. Without a word he turned and went downstairs again. Celia defied him by entering the nursery where Fiona was whimpering uncertainly, more shaken than hurt.

'I was naughty and Uncle Alan was very angry,' she confided with respect. 'He says he'll spank me again if I'm very naughty, and it hurted me.'

'I'm sure it did, darling,' said Celia, hugging her. 'We don't like Uncle Alan any more, do we?'

'Oh, yes,' Fiona corrected her aunt. 'Billy often gets spanked, but he still likes his mummy. I 'spect I was bad,' she added thoughtfully, 'but Uncle Alan said I must learn to take my—my punishment like a man. You had better go, now, Aunty, 'cause I'm in 'grace.'

Celia would have given anything to have wiped the past half hour from her remembrance, but she could not. She had an awful feeling that once again she was entirely in the wrong. Alan had administered fitting punishment and the child was neither resentful nor scarred for life.

She wondered how she could apologise and put things back to rights. No words seemed adequate, somehow, and when she remembered Alan's face as he had turned away from her she didn't relish seeking him out and making the effort at reconciliation.

Finally she decided to give him time to cool off, and when they met at dinner-time he appeared normal and happy enough. Celia knew, however, in their conversation that an intangible curtain had dropped between them. He was keeping her, most charmingly, at a distance, and her damnable pride would not permit her to barge through to reach him.

CHAPTER SIXTEEN

By Sunday evening Celia had persuaded herself that all the trouble stemmed from the fact that young Billy was at an age to lead Fiona into any kind of rascality. When Mrs Fern had agreed to come and live in the country with her small son it had seemed an excellent arrangement, but now Celia was forced to wonder if it was an arrangement which had any possibility of permanence about it. Billy would be starting at the local primary school after Christmas, whereas next year Fiona would attend a small private school. When the children attended different schools they would obviously have different friends and grow away from one another. What would be Mrs Fern's function when she was no longer required to keep an eye on Fiona?

Celia decided to broach the matter to Billy's mother without more ado. It seemed only fair to state the case while there was no real problem or need of haste.

Mrs Fern came into the house looking surprisingly flushed and pretty. Was it country air which made her look so well? She was about thirty years of age, but looked much younger at the moment with her reddish hair short and brushed high on her head. Her figure was small and neat like a schoolgirl's. Celia had to remind herself that she could be extremely tough with her small son.

'I suppose you're wondering why I sent for you, Mrs Fern, but I thought I'd better . . .'

The other regarded her watchfully.

'Well, Doctor?'

'It's difficult, and I don't want you to take this amiss. This is your home as long as you need it. But—' again Celia hesitated.

Mrs Fern flushed a dark peony shade.

'Are you trying to tell me you know?' she

asked, excitement making her voice tremble.

Celia now knew that she would do better to act as listener than speaker. Dorothy Fern obviously had something to confide.

'Perhaps you'd better tell me all about it,' Celia invited, 'whatever there is to tell.'

'Somebody's seen me with Harry, haven't they?' the woman asked happily. 'Well, you know how it is, Doctor. I never thought I could think of any man after Donald, but it happens, and now I know. I liked Harry from the start, but I never thought anything more of it until he proposed and then I knew I was in love again. He's a bit older than me, forty, with two children, the younger one ten and the older, a girl, fourteen. They quite like the idea of a new mother and we're going to spend our holidays together before the wedding. Oh, what am I saying, and what must you be thinking of me, Doctor! Harry's taken two chalets at Worthing, right on the beach, for the last two weeks in August. I was meaning to tell you, Doctor, but I wanted to be sure and I didn't want you to think I was leaving you in the lurch. You see I've been thinking that Billy does need a father. He's getting to be a handful. Also I won't be a lot of use to you much longer, and I can't occupy your flat and do nothing in return. I do hope you understand all this and don't hold anything against me?'

'Hold anything against you?' Celia echoed.

'I'm very happy for you—and Harry, too, come to that. You're not leaving anybody in the lurch and I do see what you mean about the future. One has to look ahead. When's the wedding?'

'We thought about Christmas.'

'When can I meet Harry? Can we have a little dinner-party one evening?'

'Well, Harry's a bit shy. Will you and Dr Grainger have dinner at the flat with Harry and me? I think he'd enjoy that better.'

'Very well,' Celia smiled. 'That will be nice, and we shall look forward to it.'

'There's one other thing, Doctor. About this holiday. Is it all right for me to go?'

'You must do whatever you wish.'

'Well, I wondered if Fiona could come. I would look after her and I'm sure she'd enjoy it on the beach all day long. Barbara and David are a bit old to be bothered with Billy, you see. And I know you've got your exams soon and I thought it would gve you a break.'

'That's extremely kind of you, Mrs Fern. I'll mention it to my husband and let you know.'

Alan said, in the cool, polite voice he had used ever since yesterday's débâcle, that he thought Fiona would benefit from a couple of weeks by the sea and it would, as Mrs Fern suggested, be a break for Celia.

'Mrs Borridge will also be gone those two weeks,' he remembered, 'but with the daily woman coming in you shouldn't have much to do. I would like to go off, too, about that time, if you don't mind.'

'You mean without me?'

'Actually, yes. In any case, you can't spare the time.'

'Don't bother with the afterthought. I took your point. Is your desire to get away anything to do with yesterday?'

'It is. I've been invited to lecture in the United States and have now decided to accept the invitation.'

'Is this a nice way of telling me that our marriage is on the rocks?'

He laughed mirthlessly.

'That's a dramatic way of looking at things, Celia. You are a little dramatist, though, aren't you? Let's keep to our muttons. I shall go on my lecture tour and leave you in peace to your studies for a bit. Emotional upheavals and medical facts don't make amicable bed-fellows. After my tour I shall come in again. Sometimes a second entrance makes for a more mature performance. Let's hope so, and I mean that sincerely. Meanwhile one can often see more clearly at a distance. As we are things get rather blurred on occasion, don't they, my dear?'

'Would it make any difference if I said I was sorry?' she asked humbly.

'No. But thank you, I've been waiting for that. You're sorry now, Celia, but what kind of a monster do you see in me when you're not being sorry? I can't bear to think of the creature you sometimes make me out to be, wondering if I'm Jekyll in my own sight but some horrible Hyde in yours. I think it is a good idea to pause and take stock of ourselves. This is a golden opportunity.'

'I take it you'll be gone rather longer than two weeks?'

'Nearer six.'

'Oh, Alan!' She couldn't help the pain and shock in that exclamation.

'Steady on now, Celia. If you get emotional so, I promise, shall I, and then it will all be harder to bear.'

'I feel an awful failure.'

'You're nothing of the kind. If there was nothing else to come I would still say, with my Celia was all I knew of joy and tenderness and fulfilment. If one sets such high standards the falls are bound to be a bit steep.'

She smiled tremulously.

'I hope you have a very rewarding tour. When will you be leaving?'

'The twenty-third of August. I give four lectures to post-graduate students taking vacation courses and then six more to normal undergraduates taking finals in medical-scientific subjects.'

'You'll be away for my exams.'

'That doesn't matter. You'll walk it.'

'I—I hope you're right.'

Night after night as she lay alone in the big bed—Alan automatically slept in his dressing room nowadays—her heart ached as though it was diseased. What had gone wrong, and why? She felt guilty much of the time remembering all the rows they had ever had and the reasons for them. If she made Alan out to be a monster at times, she had also succeeded in appearing one herself. Screeching insults at one's husband did not endear one to him, as had been proven. Why did she want to scream at him ever? She puzzled and puzzled until she guessed at the answer. She was unsure of Alan's true feeling for her. She felt deprived of love, which was what she secretly desired above all things.

'Feeling I never quite come up to scratch with him I do all I can to make him heed me in other ways,' she decided, 'even if it means making him utterly dislike me. I'm getting to be quite a psychiatrist in my old age. Little does Denise Raven realise how much we could do with her professional advice and how near her prediction is to coming true. She gave us a year. I wonder . . . ?'

In due course Fiona was packed off to the seaside, Mrs Borridge went off on a coach tour and Alan's own preparations for departure were omnipresent.

Celia cooked the evening meal herself, taking pleasure in providing Alan's favourite chicken curry. The pleasure was somewhat dulled when he said, 'I saw Crawley today. He was lunching at the club. He said he had seen you in town.'

Celia flushed uncomfortably. She hadn't mentioned the meeting with Tony because she simply hadn't been interested. She remembered that Alan had once asked her to tell him whenever she saw Tony. Her silence made it seem like some shady assignation.

'He said you had promised to invite him here for a meal,' Alan proceeded, 'so I told him to give you a ring while I'm away. He'll be company for you some evening.'

'Aren't you worried he might be more than company for me?' she asked sharply.

'My dear, Celia, you'll do whatever you want to do whether I'm here or not. I have at least learned something about you recently. You're too fastidious by nature to dabble in sordidness.'

Discomfited by this, Celia said, 'I say damn Tony!'

'Very well,' Alan shrugged, 'let Tony be damned. Don't upset yourself.'

Suddenly the house was empty and lonely and crying out in the night. Celia dared think about nothing but her coming examinations and her work by day. Dr Wilkes-Mather teased her, 'I'll have to offer you a partnership if you get it, you know.'

'I shall have a long nervous breakdown

first,' Celia replied.

She was feeling tired these days and rather peculiar. She felt dizzy on rising in the mornings, and one day she couldn't get to the bathroom quickly enough to vomit. Afterwards she felt perfectly normal and much relieved.

'I must have eaten something which disagreed with me,' she decided, and went off to Harley Street without more ado, something else by this time on her mind.

The next morning, however, it happened again, a desire to go and vomit rather than an actual vomiting, and afterwards she again felt quite normal. When it happened a third time, however, she regarded her perspiring face in the bathroom mirror, a question written all over her countenance.

Could she be . . . ? No, it wasn't possible . . . it was possible although highly improbable . . . weren't they two doctors and supposed to know all about these things . . . ? But nature played these tricks on a woman quite often. There was no guarantee against its happening. So she could, just possibly, be pregnant against all their contriving.

'Good lord!' she exclaimed. The thought had made her feel temporarily faint. 'No, it must be something else. Flatulence, possibly. I'm not eating enough or regularly. This is a warning and I must take heed.'

When the same thing happened the following two mornings, however, she took her head out of the sand and faced things squarely.

'I'm pregnant, and there it is. Not only am I pregnant but I must be about six weeks advanced, judging by the morning sickness.' She began to laugh weakly. It was Saturday and she was all alone as even the daily woman did not come in at weekends, so she could afford to think about her condition. 'Trust me to start a baby just when my husband has decided he's sick of me,' she pondered wryly. 'There's a complication for us!'

That day Tony phoned suggesting he should come over for a cosy chat.

'Sorry, Tony, not today. I'm going out.'

She went out and worked in the garden, to make this statement true, but later she had a lonely little dinner, thinking all the time of how she was missing Alan and wondering what he was doing. When he was leaving he had said, 'I won't write, Celia, if you don't mind, and then you can keep plugging away at your books without distractions. Letters are a rotten substitute, anyway. If there's any emergency this address will find me, but please—' he had paused to smile reminiscently—'don't let Fiona burn the house down while I'm gone!'

Somehow, although she tried to interest herself in megaloblastic anaemias, her mind kept reverting to her condition. With luck she should be able to sit for her examinations in their entirety before she became at all ungainly. She would be nine weeks pregnant when she sat for the written work and twelve or fourteen weeks at the oral and clinical examinations, providing she passed the first part, that was. At the swearing-in ceremony she would just be starting to show a little, but what matter? She was a married woman, and it would be a doubly proud occasion for her.

What would Alan have to say about it?

Oh, he mustn't know, not yet. She didn't want him to feel he must endure her society because she was, owing to some blunder, carrying his child in her. The thought made her feel cosy, suddenly. His child. Alan's flesh and blood was warm somewhere within her. They hadn't been able to keep that little morsel out despite their planning and precautions.

'Of course I've got to pass my exams this time as I'll be too involved for the next year or two,' she suddenly panicked, and forced her attention back to her books with a tremendous effort at concentration.

CHAPTER SEVENTEEN

The next few weeks consisted of a few stark incidents with all that was at stake in Celia's life at the moment. Her household had assembled around her again, apart from Alan, and was functioning normally. She was like a separate entity living in a private world of her own. Everybody respectfully kept clear, and eventually she sailed into the examination room on that golden September day, looked at the set papers and breathed in relief.

She wrote fluently, quickly. There were fourteen candidates for Membership and some would fail. Maybe she would be one of them. She knew the subjects she had chosen to write on, but it was difficult to know the standards on which the expositions would be judged. Still, it was a relief to be actually doing the examination rather than anticipating it. Alan's telegram burned in her brain. THE VERY BEST OF LUCK FOR TODAY, it said. For him it was that she assembled her facts, lined them up in order of importance, sought out turns of phrase to embellish the whole and finally handed in the foolscap sheets with a conviction that if what she had done was not good enough then she was incapable of doing better.

A month later, successful in her first

attempt, she presented herself for the oral and clinical examinations of parts two and three of the Membership examinations. These were spread over the best part of a week, and she did not feel as happy or confident as a month ago.

This was partly due to the fact that her heart was screaming out for Alan's return and had suffered a bitter disappointment. A further telegram from him had read: AM ASKED TO EXTEND TOUR BY TWO WEEKS STOP DO YOU WANT ME BACK IMMEDIATELY.

It only needed for Celia to cry 'Come!' to bring him back by the very next plane, but that same pride which had always prevented emotional declarations between them now made her believe that he really wanted to extend his tour but felt guilty about doing so. Her reply was typical. ALL WELL HERE STOP DO STAY ON AS LONG AS YOU WISH, which, when Alan received it, made his mouth turn down in a wry little grimace which was this man's way of demonstrating the deepest of hurts.

Celia's confidence was also undermined by the fact that she was not feeling very well. She had suffered a slight haemorrhage on the day of the orals which had, fortunately, cleared up, so she didn't mention it to anybody. But she was worried about it, hoping it meant no harm to the child she was carrying. Once the clinicals were safely over she could have a day or two in bed and coddle herself. For that she was really longing. She was feeling quite exhausted.

How she got through the clinicals she never afterwards knew. Sharp, griping pains were gripping her vitals at intervals. Fortunately the treatments she was asked to perform came to her like second nature, but it was as though she was a divided person. One part of her felt as if it was dying and the other was answering questions and bandaging and dressing and diagnosing as though nothing was amiss.

She almost cried in relief when the last of her examiners said, 'Well done, Doctor!' and it was all over. In the women's cloakroom there was the shrill chatter of other relieved examinees, but this washed over Celia's head like a receding tide. She had difficulty finding her coat, remembering if she had brought one or not, and all the while there was pain and nausea and a detached conviction that the world might end at any moment.

'I say,' a voice pierced into her consciousness for a moment, 'is anything wrong? You look terrible, my dear.'

Celia swam to the surface to regard an anxious face with large horn-rimmed spectacles regarding her. There was silence, now, in the cloakroom; other anxious faces.

'I think I need help,' Celia said quietly, and swayed as pain drowned her again.

'Oh, my God!' was the last thing she heard

before she slid to the floor. 'Get help, quickly! The poor thing's aborting, or something terrible.'

★ ★ ★

For the first time in what appeared to be eternity, Celia opened her eyes and there was no pain. There was a feeling of discomfort, but it was pure relief after what had passed, and as it had been such an effort to lift leaden eyelids she knew it was, at present, beyond her physical powers to lift so much as a finger.

With a certain amount of interest she regarded the upended vacolitre of blood feeding into a vein in her left arm, the needle neatly sealed beneath a band of Elastoplast. How often in the past had she opened up a vein and started a transfusion, but to be on the receiving end of such ministrations was certainly a novelty.

The door opened and a smiling, plump-faced Sister came in and put her finger on Celia's limp wrist.

'Well, that's better, Mrs Grainger,' she said happily. 'Much, much better.'

Celia pondered that if this terrible lassitude was better what must she have been like when she was bad? She mentioned this, fuzzily, and the woman laughed.

'You're under sedation, dear. Got to keep

quiet. You had a nasty time. But we managed to save the baby.'

Celia's heart tried to leap, but she was too sedated even for that.

'The baby's still all right?' she asked, disbelievingly.

'Yes. It was touch and go, but we did it. Now let me tidy you up, because you've got a visitor. It's really much too early, but we can't keep him out any longer.'

'Dear old Wilkes-Mather,' Celia thought affectionately. 'They told him and he's deserted the practice to come and see me.'

But it was Alan who came through the doorway, glared at the Sister as though she was his mortal enemy and then sank on his knees by the bedside with a little strangled cry and laid his cheek against the transparent little hand on the coverlet.

'Alan?' she inquired after a long moment, wondering if he was ever going to speak.

'Alan,' she said, 'I'm all right, you know. I'm not going to die, and the baby's still here. I suppose they told you about the baby?'

'Damn the baby!' was torn from him.

She knew he didn't mean this and a little smile trembled on her pallid lips.

'They brought you back from your tour,' she ventured regretfully.

'Damn my tour!' was all the response she got to this.

Finally he was able to raise his head and

regard her. His lips were still tremulous and she could see all the pain which had ground her down somehow etched upon his countenance.

'Celia, it was wrong to go away and leave you. I did it for you, so there would be no more rows to distract you, but I couldn't stick it. You were everywhere I went, in my shaving mirror, in my suitcase . . . I just can't live without you, and there it is. I've accepted the fact. That very first day I saw you I fell head over heels in love with you. I resisted it like hell, because look where it got me last time. I thought I would try for a more permanent relationship with you, if I could interest you, and build this marriage on rock. But I seem to have made a mess of it; I haven't been able to satisfy you and make you happy. Please say you'll let me try again, that you'll have patience with me . . . ?'

Her hand ran through the dark hair lying against the coverlet.

'Darling Alan, haven't we both been barking up the wrong tree all this time? You say you fell in love with me. So did I with you, long before you appeared even to notice me. Why should the heart be such a bad old spokesman after all? Knowing that we love each other, do the fights matter? We'll have them—get over them. If only I'd known how you felt! But there's no time for any more "if onlys." You mentioned a second entrance

239

before you went away. Can I start again, too? I love you so much, Alan, that I care only about you. I merely wanted my Membership to make you proud of me.'

He took her gently in arms strong as steel and whispered into her ear.

'You're the loveliest wife a man ever had, Celia, and I am proud of you, Membership or no. I have a confession to make. I lied to you. Nobody asked me to stay on in America, but I wanted to hear you say "Come on back, all is forgiven." When you didn't I caught the next plane back, anyway, not knowing the merry hell I was to find with police cars waiting at the airport and you in this place. I've been here two whole days. Did you know that? Made myself enemies for life with the obstetric team by demanding they remove this child you managed to conceive behind my back. How you did it I'll never know, but I suppose I'll get used to the idea in time.'

She was smiling and very happy. Even a little colour crept into her lips as he lightly kissed them.

'All's well that ends well,' she said softly.

'Ends, my darling?' he queried this. 'Perhaps you're right. Let's call this the end of the beginning and go on from here. It wasn't so bad in parts, was it, for two people so determined not to be hoodwinked by mere emotions?'

'After this I'll respect my mere emotions,'

Celia promised. 'When you spend a night at the flat in future I'll be there, too, so I warn you.'

'And very welcome,' he told her. 'I won't stay unless you are.'

'And your dressing room is a dressing room only. Understand?'

He looked at her with admiring respect.

'What you achieved without really trying already amazes me, wife of mine,' there was a wicked twinkle in the dark eyes which thrilled her through all the sedation, 'but I can see you're really going to ask for it in future.'

'But if I have got my Membership, and I feel lucky in my bones today, shouldn't we well-diplomaed types lead the way in having big, intellectual families?'

He said, with a sealing kiss, 'Just babies, my own love. I'll settle for babies.'

Sister Perivale came bustling in, smiling indulgently on the pair, and began to dismantle the transfusion apparatus.

'I really think you'll do now, Mrs Grainger,' she remarked, unheard. 'It looks to me as though you'll do.'

Photoset, printed and bound in Great Britain by
REDWOOD BURN LIMITED, Trowbridge, Wiltshire

LT V791La c.1

Vinton, Anne.

Lady in Harley Street

TC9625 $13.95

JAN. 18 1997
JAN. 21 1997
JE24 '97